MYSTERY OF THE SCAR

By the same author:

Child of Destiny
Escape from the Darkness

Mystery of the Scar

CONNIE GRIFFITH

AFRICA EVANGELICAL FELLOWSHIP

KINGSWAY PUBLICATIONS

EASTBOURNE

This book is published in conjunction with the
Africa Evangelical Fellowship
35 Kingfisher Court, Hambridge Road,
Newbury RG14 5SJ, UK.

Front cover design by Vic Mitchell

British Library Cataloguing in Publication Data

Griffith, Connie
    Mystery of the scar.
    I. Title   II. series
    813.54

    ISBN 0-86065-597-0

Printed in Great Britain for
KINGSWAY PUBLICATIONS LTD
1 St Anne's Road, Eastbourne, E Sussex BN21 3UN by
Courier International Ltd, Tiptree, Essex
Typeset by Watermark, Norfolk House, Cromer

Dedicated to my parents,
Arleigh and Vivian Kringle,
who love unconditionally.
Faithful service is their hallmark.

This story is the conclusion of the
Tales of Muniamma series, continuing from
Child of Destiny and *Escape from the Darkness*

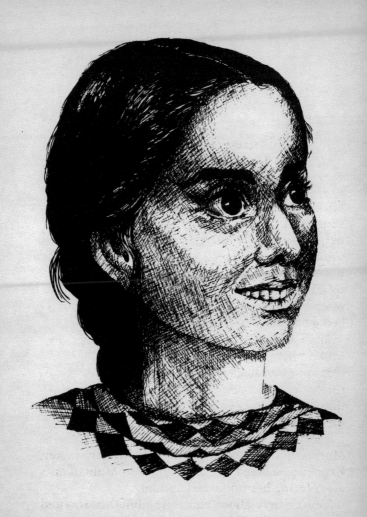

Chapter One

Muniamma looked at the gathering crowd on the shore and, once again, her stomach twisted into a tight knot. She and Grandmother were standing some distance away, waist-deep in the waves. Muni felt chilled as the cool evening breeze whipped splashes of sea water over her skinny body. Grandmother had just come up out of the water after being baptised. It was Muni's turn next.

Missionary Morton and her uncle stepped forward to help.

Muni could hear her dog growling at the edge of the crowd and even from that distance she could see that Sparky was baring his teeth and about to attack the person hiding in the shadows.

Everyone turned and as the crowd moved aside Muniamma immediately recognised her father, Krish. He seemed to glare right into Muniamma's eyes, daring her not to be baptised.

'Don't worry about him,' Grandmother shouted above the noise of the waves. 'I know he's made your life miserable, mine too. But now is not the time to let your father frighten you.'

'But Ma, what about Father's plan for me to marry that awful partner of his?'

'Don't worry, child. You'll see—everything will work out. We are Christians now, and God will protect us.'

Suddenly an old woman screeched, 'Eeech!' Her eerie scream pierced the air. 'Eeech! Whoever heard of Hindus turning Christians? You were born a Hindu, you will die a Hindu!' She picked up a stone and threw it with all her might. The old woman looked frail, but the rock soared through the air and narrowly missed Muniamma's arm.

'Oh Ma,' Muni wailed. 'I'm scared! I can't go through with this! I'm not like you, I'm not a strong enough Christian.'

'Nonsense, child.'

'Listen to your grandmother,' Mr Morton said. He and Muniamma's uncle were standing beside her, each ready to take her arm and dunk her.

'That's right!' Uncle said. 'There's no need for you to be frightened. You've got a heavenly Father who loves you dearly.'

Just then a particularly large wave pounded over them, and Muniamma stumbled backwards, trying her best to retain her balance. Salt water poured into her eyes and mouth. She could still hear the old woman screeching and Sparky barking.

Desperately she pulled away and began running, arms thrashing and water splashing everywhere, stumbling headlong through the surf. But when she finally reached the beach she ran as if the devil himself were chasing her.

Muniamma moved so fast that for the moment everyone remained rooted to the spot in surprise— all except for Sparky, who started running down the beach after her. But as soon as Krish turned to leave, everyone began talking at the same time.

Several hours later, Muniamma was still hiding, crouching low behind an old crumbling tombstone.

'Oh Sparky,' she whispered. 'What is going to happen to me? I can't go back. I can't face anybody. And I certainly don't ever want to see my father or his awful partner again! I just can't stand it a minute longer.'

Sparky squirmed out of Muniamma's grasp and backed away.

'Don't leave me now, boy. I need you more than ever.'

'Over this way.' It was Uncle's voice, and he was leading the search. He sounded much closer than Muniamma had thought, and her eyes pleaded with Sparky to remain silent.

'I'm sure I heard that dog of hers,' Uncle continued. 'Shine your torches over to the right.'

'Good gracious!' someone exclaimed. 'It's a graveyard. Muniamma certainly wouldn't be hiding in there.' It was Grandmother Poonamah's voice. Muni was surprised her old Ma was out with the others, scouring the hills around Isipingo. Muniamma felt a twinge of guilt. Lately, she and Ma had become friends, and Muni didn't want to do anything to destroy these new feelings. But she knew she simply could not face anyone yet; not even Grandmother.

11

Whoever was holding the torch turned away from the graves and directed the beam toward Grandmother. Muni peeped out from around the tombstone. Ma's short form was wrapped in a wool blanket, and her dark brown face was creased with worry. Wiry grey hair stuck out in all directions.

For an instant, Muniamma wanted to cry, 'Ma, I'm over here. Come!' But she didn't. Instead, she pulled back and held on to Sparky. As always, her faithful dog seemed to sense her need, and he silently nestled closer.

'Well Poonamah,' Uncle said hesitantly to Ma. 'Maybe we should look behind all these tombstones, just in case.' Then he hesitated, 'On second thoughts, maybe we shouldn't. Maybe we should skirt this graveyard and look on the other side.' His voice sounded strained, and Muniamma felt more miserable than ever.

'This looks like a Hindu burial ground and I definitely don't want to go through it,' someone from the crowd said.

'I can't believe my ears,' Mr Morton exclaimed. 'It sounds as if you're scared. There's nothing in this graveyard that can harm you. Come on—let's search the whole area.'

No one budged. Behind the tombstone, Muniamma stiffened as if frozen in place. The tense silence continued. Finally Uncle spoke. 'You are not from around here, Pastor Morton. You are from England where things must be different. We are Asian Indians in South Africa. We have been Hindus most of our lives, and we are well aware of

12

spiritual battles.'

'But you are Christians now,' the missionary frowned. 'I honestly don't understand why you are still so fearful.'

Uncle straightened to his full height. 'I don't believe we're afraid. I would say we are cautious. We don't want to run headlong into evil forces if it is not absolutely necessary.'

Everyone nodded.

Muniamma shivered.

Aunt Sita was among the searchers and she stepped forward and stood next to Uncle. A few strands of black hair had escaped her neat bun and they whipped around her face in the cool night breeze. She self-consciously adjusted her sari and said in a respectful tone, 'I really don't believe Muniamma would be hiding here among the graves.'

The missionary shook his head. 'If you two feel this way, and all the rest of you do too,' he said, looking at the search party, 'then certainly the child is nowhere near here. But honestly, I don't understand. I'd have thought you would be more concerned about that ruthless father of hers than about the spirits of the dead.'

'We *are* concerned about Krish,' Uncle interrupted. 'And we must find Muniamma before he does.'

The people in the search party mumbled among themselves. Muni peeped out again. Aunt Sita was wringing her hands, 'I must admit that I'm terribly worried about Krish and what he will do to

Muniamma, but I'm also deeply concerned about Krish's partner. And, who knows, maybe even that old Hindu woman who kept screeching taunts at the baptism is a serious threat.'

Uncle stepped forward. 'Sita is right. We haven't seen the last of any of them. But first, we must find Muniamma, and I don't think she's here. Let's go around to the other side. We'll split up and scour the whole countryside. Let's meet back at my home in Isipingo in one hour.'

Muniamma could hear Uncle's concerned voice as he continued giving instructions. But by now they had walked away so she could not distinguish all his words. Muni did not want them to leave, yet she could not face them either. Her actions at the baptismal service had been disgraceful, and she knew she had embarrassed her grandmother, the whole missionary family and the rest of the Christians. She had made a complete fool of herself. 'How can Grandmother be so brave as a brand-new Christian?' Muni asked herself again, 'when I'm so scared?'

She hugged Sparky, and her wet dress clung to her thin body; goose flesh covered every inch of her bony back. Sparky licked her soft brown face and even his tongue sent new chills up and down her. Muni's wet hair fell like a thickly braided rope to her shoulder and around her neck. She flicked it away and it hung heavy down her back, almost to her waist.

'Why is my life so miserable?' she sobbed silently into Sparky's neck. His thick black fur had been cropped short and the prickly new growth felt

14

strange. Even his bad breath, as he panted in her face, brought no warmth.

'It's just you and me again, boy,' she whispered to her dog. She held his loving head between both hands, and they stared at one another. The moon was bright and Muni could see his big face clearly. Sparky's eyes were filled with water and there was dirt in the corners. 'I'm scared!' she admitted breathlessly. 'Oh why didn't I let Ma and Uncle and Aunt Sita find me?'

A strange noise came from the other side of the graveyard. Leaves rustled and Muni felt certain she heard someone take a step. *It's a spirit from the dead,* she thought and stifled a scream. She pushed her face into Sparky's neck and prickly black hair filled her gaping mouth.

That noise again.

'Help me, God!' Muniamma cried silently. 'Don't let an evil spirit get me.' In that instant, the past few years flashed before her. The visions brought new terror, and she bit down hard. Sparky yelped.

That noise again.

'Help!' Muniamma screamed at the top of her lungs. Her terrified voice echoed back and forth around the graves. It sounded weird, even to her own ears.

'Who's there?' she tried to yell, but her voice came out in a tiny squeak. 'Is...is someone over there?'

Muniamma waited. Silence.

'Are you a spirit from the dead?' she whispered into the eerie stillness. And then a thought, almost more terrifying, surfaced. 'Are...er...are you my

15

father? Have you and that other horrible man come to get me?'

Nothing.

The strain was too much, and Muniamma stumbled to her feet and began running. Sparky barked wildly and darted after her. Muni heard footsteps closing in, and she ran faster. As soon as the cemetery was behind her, she began scrambling up the hill which separated her from the town of Isipingo and from safety. She felt certain the search party could not be far away; surely they would hear her screams and come to her rescue.

'Help!' Muniamma tried to scream, but this time no voice came. She tried again. Her lips were parched, and an acid taste filled her mouth. With tears streaming down her face and her breath coming in ragged gasps, she kept running. Sparky had passed her and was already at the top of the hill, barking.

Suddenly Muniamma fell. She did not know what had happened, but the last thing she remembered was a haze of pain in her head. Then blackness.

Chapter Two

The Morton twins were visiting Muniamma's aunt and uncle's house; nervously they paced back and forth in the bedroom.

'Why won't Mum let us help?' Sue whined. She stamped her foot and clenched her fists. 'Muniamma's our friend. It's just not fair!'

Lou kept pacing but she did not speak.

'You'd think we were children by the way we're treated. We're fourteen. But oh no...do you think that's old enough to help?' Sue's short blonde curls bobbed up and down as she shook her head in frustration. 'Do something! Say something, Lou! You can't just take this treatment and do nothing. . .and neither can I.'

Lou stopped and looked at her twin. 'What can we do? You know Mum forbade us to go. She absolutely refuses to let us join the search party.'

'But we must do *something*. I bet if we were boys she would let us go.'

Lou looked away and started pacing again. 'You know she wouldn't. She didn't let Kenny go.'

This didn't stop Sue. 'No, but where is our big

brother now? I don't see him in here pacing the floor.'

'I don't know where Kenny is, but he certainly wouldn't disobey Mum.'

'Oh sure!' Sue said sarcastically, and hit her fist against the palm of her hand. Then silence reigned once again between the twins. The ticking of the old-fashioned clock on Aunt Sita's bedside table seemed to pound into Sue's head. She went over and picked up the clock. She felt like throwing it against the wall but decided instead to bury it under a couple of pillows.

'It's ten o'clock! Oh Lou, what's happened to Muniamma? Why haven't they found her?'

Lou plopped down on the saggy mattress. Her breaths came in nervous little catches. 'I don't know. Do you think her father has found her?'

'Oh, that awful man!' Sue exploded again. 'Have you ever known someone so hateful? I've never heard of anything like this in England.'

Lou looked up at her distraught twin. 'What do you think made him like this? I mean, he is her father, and I've never heard of anyone hating his own daughter.'

'I don't know what has filled him with such hate and I don't care. But I'm scared he's going to find Muniamma before the search party does. And I absolutely can't bear the thought of him forcing Muni to marry that terrible partner of his!'

Both girls felt sickened by that possibility and they stared into each other's light brown eyes. They were picturing Krish's fat partner with his

18

tight-fitting clothes, and they shuddered in revulsion.

Lou asked with a nervous catch in her voice, 'He can't make Muniamma marry such a man, can he?'

'No, of course not,' Sue quickly responded, but she did not sound at all convincing.

Again they both began to pace. The long minutes dragged by. Finally Sue interrupted their thoughts. 'I wonder what made Muniamma so scared today that she ran away instead of being baptised? Her grandmother was brave enough to go through with it. After all that Muniamma has endured, you would think a little baptismal service would be nothing.'

'Who knows? Maybe it was that old toothless woman who kept threatening Grandma Poonamah and Muni while they were being baptised that scared her. But, whatever the case, Muniamma must have had enough. She's probably feeling afraid and ashamed. But she needn't,' Lou continued with conviction. 'No one's going to blame her for getting scared. Honestly, I don't know anyone who has gone through as much as Muni. She's been super.'

'What do you think the Hindus are going to say?'

'Frankly, Sue, I don't care. All I care about is Muniamma!'

'Well, me too. But I was just wondering.'

Unexpectedly, they heard a tapping at the window. For a moment they stared at each other, and then Sue ran to the window and pulled back the patterned curtain.

It was Kenny, standing outside with his friend, Raneesh, who lived next door. The boys motioned for Sue to open the window.

'What are you doing out there?' Lou exclaimed, as she and Sue stuck their heads out.

Ken's straight brown hair hung into his eyes. 'We're going to search for Muniamma. Come with us.'

'But you can't go, and neither can we,' Lou said to her brother. 'And what about you, Raneesh? Do your parents know you're out looking for Muni?'

'Oh, mind your own business!' Sue whispered hoarsely, totally exasperated. 'Who cares about getting permission at a time like this?'

'Yeah,' Ken interjected.

Lou was not put off. 'Raneesh, you know your parents are still Hindus, and they're watching everything you do. It would be awful if you did something that really upset them.'

Raneesh nodded thoughtfully. 'Thank you for your concern.' His brown skin shone in the moonlight. Even with his wavy, coconut-oiled hair all tousled, he looked handsome. 'But my parents do know I'm with Ken. I didn't tell them what we were going to do, but...'

Ken interrupted. 'For pity's sake, Lou. Stop being such a confounded busybody and leave Raneesh alone!'

'I agree,' Sue snapped. Then she looked at Ken. 'I'm glad you and Raneesh are at least doing something. We've been in here, pacing the floor.'

Raneesh stepped closer to the window so that his face was only just below the twins'. 'I'm certain you girls have also been praying. For a long time Ken and I have been sitting out here under the tree bringing this problem to God.'

Lou and Sue felt ashamed. They hadn't even thought of praying.

Ken looked a little embarrassed but slightly smug. 'That's right, we've been praying. And now Raneesh thinks we ought to go and look around.'

'But you can't, Kenny,' Lou once again reminded her brother. 'Mum said to stay here. She told you not to join the search party.'

'He's not joining the search party,' Sue said in an utterly exasperated tone. 'He and Raneesh are looking for Muniamma on their own. And I'm joining them.'

Quickly she pulled up her yellow gingham skirt and swung one leg over the window sill. She was straddling the edge, ready to pull the other leg through and jump when Ken said, 'Slow up, Sis. It's a short drop, but be careful.'

Sue ignored her brother, and just as she was about to jump, her sandal caught on the small bush below the window. She went sprawling to the ground. Angrily she got up, dusted off the reddish dirt and grabbed her sandal from where it still hung in the stubby branches.

'Well, Lou, what are you waiting for?' Sue said, trying desperately to regain her dignity. 'Are you coming with us?'

21

Lou hung out of the window, 'Gosh, are you all right?'

'Yeah. Hurry! We shan't find Muniamma at this rate.'

'I don't know,' Lou faltered. 'I still think we shouldn't go. You know what Mum said.'

'Oh shut up!' Sue and Ken said at the same time.

Raneesh looked completely miserable. 'I didn't know your mother told you not to join in the search. To disobey would not be right. I agree with Lou. We had better not go.'

Both Ken and Sue glared at Lou.

'Mum didn't exactly forbid it,' Ken defended. 'And besides, Raneesh, aren't you and Muniamma becoming friends? You don't want that father of hers finding her before we do...or what about his partner?'

'That's right,' Sue added. 'We've got to do something. They might get to her first.'

Distraught, Raneesh walked away from the others and kicked at some dried clumps of mud. He thrust his hands into the pockets of his light jacket and circled around the nearby tree.

The three Mortons waited in silence.

Raneesh did not know what to do. He had always tried to obey his parents, especially since he had become a Christian. To an Indian youth, showing respect to parents was of utmost importance. He knew in his own heart that they would be angry if their son went out looking for the Christian girl who had run away from the baptismal service. They had laughed, along with the

22

other Hindus, when Muniamma ran and hid. They had not forbidden him to search for her, but he knew they expected him to remain near home.

Ken became impatient. 'Well...what are we going to do? Are we going or not?'

'Of course we are!' Sue added. 'But we'll leave Lou here. She can pray for us.'

Lou couldn't tell if Sue was making fun or not.

Raneesh never got a chance to answer. His parents, Mr and Mrs Naidoo, shouted from their back door. 'Raneesh...Raneesh, school's tomorrow, and you need to get to bed—it's already past ten.'

Raneesh waited. He kicked another clump of dried mud.

'Where is that boy?' his mother called.

'He'd better not be up to any mischief,' Mr Naidoo added. 'I think those Christians are a bad influence on him, especially those white children from England. They act so carefree, as if life isn't serious.'

Every one of the eaves-dropping teenagers felt embarrassed, even Sue.

Raneesh hurried away from his missionary friends before his parents could say any more. 'Here I am,' he answered loudly and clearly. 'I'm coming!'

Ken and the twins remained uncomfortably still until the Naidoos were safely inside their small home. Then Sue whispered angrily, 'What do they mean...we're a bad influence? And of course we take life seriously! We've been doing nothing all evening except worry about Muniamma.'

Neither Ken nor Lou responded, which was strange, and this made Sue even more upset.

'Well, we're not Indians,' Sue said emphatically. 'Why can't these people just accept us for who we are? Good grief, we've come all the way across the sea to help them! We're not bad; we're just different.'

'Maybe we should all be more careful,' Ken suggested.

This subdued nature in her brother was new, and Sue didn't like it. 'Now don't go all weird on us, Kenny. There is nothing wrong with having fun once in a while.'

'I know,' Ken agreed.

'And besides, just because we go around with smiles and laughter instead of long drawn-out faces, doesn't mean we are a bad influence. I thought we were being good influences.'

'Me too,' Ken said. 'But tonight, I don't want to go and look for Muniamma, not any more. I guess the excitement has just been knocked out of it.'

'Good grief!' Sue exclaimed, but Lou thought she detected a slight tone of relief in her sister's voice.

With Lou and Ken's help, Sue climbed back into the bedroom and Ken followed.

After a little while of awkward silence, Ken said almost sheepishly, 'Maybe the best thing we can do right now is forget about being misunderstood and pray for Muniamma.'

'I guess it's the only thing we can do,' Lou added,

pleased and surprised at her brother's response.

All three Mortons looked at each other and nodded.

'Yes,' Sue agreed reluctantly. 'Only God can help Muniamma now.'

Chapter Three

Muniamma's forehead hit a low branch of a huge jacaranda tree in her flight up the hill. Dozens of purple blossoms fell with her, and now they lay strewn everywhere like flowers arranged around a dead body.

Sparky dashed back to where she lay and barked wildly. He took a mouthful of Muniamma's damp sleeve and began pulling. The dress tore. He then pushed his nose into her face and sniffed the blood which oozed from the gash above her left eye. Sparky was still whining when two men approached.

'I'm glad this tree stopped her before I had to,' Muni's father said to his fat partner. They laughed, and the sound was wicked.

Sparky turned and growled, baring his teeth. The growl issued from deep in his throat.

'You stupid animal...get out of our way!' Krish kicked Sparky and hit him in the ribs. Sparky yelped, but did not move.

'Hey, Krish,' the partner scowled. 'We've had our plans ruined before. Do something right this time!'

Krish glared at his partner, then down at the mad dog and over to the pathetic form of his helpless daughter. No love filled his heart at all; not for anyone but himself. His thin, dark brown face turned almost black with pent-up anger and hate. His greasy hair hung into his eyes, and he pushed it out of the way.

'Yeah, I'll do it right this time,' Krish spat out each word. 'You can count on it. When she comes to, I'm going to tell her she has to marry you. She'll have nothing whatsoever to say in the matter.'

'Now you're talking. If I'm going to set us up in business, then at least you have to come through with your side of the bargain and give me your daughter in marriage.'

Krish's partner, Raj, had a huge belly that hung over his belt. His shirt was open almost to his waist and a gold medallion nestled in his hairy chest. In spite of the cool evening breeze, he was sweating profusely. He looked down at Muniamma's crumpled form.

'Shake her. Make her come around!' he demanded of Krish. 'At least I want a good look at my bride before we wed.' He slapped Krish along the shoulder and laughed again.

Krish stumbled and Sparky growled.

'I hear she has a lot of pluck,' Raj continued. 'Is it true she ran away before those Christians could baptise her?'

'Yeah.'

'I like it...I like it. I like pluck in a woman.'

'She's only thirteen.'

'Good!'

For a brief moment, Krish felt uneasy. He did not like the look in his partner's eyes. These feelings quickly vanished, however, as he visualised the illegal drinking-place his partner's money would buy. 'I need that money,' he said to himself. 'Finally my daughter will bring me a little luck, and my life will turn around. I deserve some good fortune.'

Just then Muniamma began to stir. She moaned several times, and Sparky's barking became more intense.

'Get out of here, you stupid animal!' Krish demanded and picked up a stick to swing at the dog. Sparky yelped and whined, but Krish kept hitting him.

'Stop,' Muniamma cried weakly. 'Leave my dog alone!' She tried to sit, but fell back into the dried leaves and purple flowers. 'Run, Sparky,' Muni sobbed. 'Don't let them hurt you.'

'Don't worry your pretty little head, lovey. I'm not going to let your father hurt your precious dog.'

Muniamma's stomach heaved. Even Krish stopped and stared at his partner in disbelief. 'What's got into you? Why all the sudden sweet-talk?'

Krish's fat partner grinned. 'This is the first time I'm having a good look at my bride-to-be. Well, well, she's a pretty little thing. I hope that gash on her forehead doesn't leave a scar. Introduce us, Krish. We haven't been properly introduced.'

'If I can get this stupid dog to stop yapping for a second, maybe we can hear ourselves talk.' Krish kicked Sparky several more times and finally chased him away.

'Go and get help,' Muniamma cried after him.

All the while, that sickening Raj just kept staring at Muni. She managed to sit up, but she could not trust her legs yet.

Krish turned at the top of the hill and came back towards them. He was out of breath by the time he reached them, and he hauled Muni roughly to her feet. 'There's no help coming,' he sneered. 'We've got you now. Daughter, this is Raj. He's going to be your husband.'

'Never!' Muniamma cried. She shook off his hand and stood tall. She straightened her dress the best she could. Her head throbbed, and she wiped some of the sticky blood off her face.

'Don't speak to me like that. You will do as I say. I'm your father, and I demand obedience.'

'You haven't been a father to me,' Muniamma cried. She was shocked at her own boldness. 'You ran away the day I was born. How can you come back into my life now and tell me what to do?' Muniamma wiped her forehead with the back of her hand again, and the blood from the gash smeared her skin.

'I can and I will tell you what to do!' Krish was getting more angry by the minute, and he began slobbering with each word. 'You are lucky to get a man like Raj; he will treat you right.'

Raj smiled and once again Muniamma's stomach heaved.

'I will never marry this man,' she shouted.

'Now, now, lovey, don't get so upset; it ruins your

pretty looks.' Raj stepped near and put his sweaty arm around her.

She wrenched free and stumbled backwards. 'I can't marry such a man,' she cried, and her whole body began quaking. Screwing up her face as if her mouth was stuffed with something sour, she screamed at Raj, 'Never! Never will I marry you!'

Raj's eyes became like narrow slits. Beads of perspiration glistened across the dark pores of his puffy face. With obvious lust he slowly looked Muniamma up and down.

Muni covered her face and began sobbing. She felt filthy. Minutes passed while Raj kept staring at her with evil desire.

Krish became uneasy and slapped Raj on the back, 'Hey, man. She'll be yours soon enough. I'm giving her to you as your bride.'

'I know,' Raj said, not taking his eyes off Muni. 'You're giving me this beautiful thing in exchange for money.'

Put so bluntly, the deal sounded dreadful. Krish wiped his brow with the back of his dirty rolled-up sleeve and began shifting his weight from one foot to the other. *She is my daughter*, he thought. *But she's brought nothing but bad luck. Oh how I wish she'd never been born.*

Muniamma couldn't stand up any longer. Suddenly she crumpled to the ground like a rag doll and cried into the earth, 'Go away...I hate you! I'll never marry you as long as I live!'

Raj leaned back and laughed. 'She's got lots of pluck! We're going to have good times together.'

Muniamma looked up, and her huge brown eyes appeared strangely lost among her delicate features. Blood from the gash started rolling down her cheek, mingling with her tears, but she didn't seem to notice. Dirt and a few purple blossoms hung in her hair, and they were swiftly brushed aside as Muniamma flicked her long, thick braid over her shoulder. She looked directly at Raj. 'You're ugly! You are...you are big and fat and...and mean!'

When she saw the change in expression on Raj's face she knew she had gone too far. She couldn't believe she'd said all that to an adult, not even to someone as horrible as her father's partner.

'Hey, man,' Krish said as he, too, noticed the drastic change in Raj's attitude. 'She doesn't mean it. She's upset. And besides, like I've said before, you're a handsome man and my daughter will be lucky to have you as a husband!'

Raj took a step towards Krish. 'You bet she'll be lucky to get me. Women have always found me attractive. I like pluck, but I won't take insults.' Raj lifted his shoulders and his huge flabby belly wobbled back and forth.

'Hey, man, like I said, she doesn't mean it.' There was desperation in Krish's tone.

Muniamma wanted to scream, 'I *do* mean it,' but after her last outburst all she could do was lie on the ground and whimper.

Raj walked over and stood directly above Muniamma's crumpled form. She couldn't stop her body from shaking. Seconds passed, and the tension

31

mounted. Finally Raj spoke and his voice was low, 'Krish, here's my deal. I'll give you the money you need for your business, but you must give me this daughter of yours, and she must come to me as a willing and respectful bride.'

Krish leaped forward with clenched fists, 'You can't be serious.'

'That's the deal. Take it or leave it. She must come to me showing deep respect.'

'But how am I going to make my daughter change her mind?' Krish's hatred increased. His whole life had been a failure, and he'd grown used to blaming Muniamma for everything.

Raj's laugh was low and wicked, 'There are ways, Krish. There are ways to make people change their minds. I'm walking away from you for the second time, and I'm warning you, don't come to me again unless you bring me this daughter of yours with a willing and ready smile.'

All the time Raj was speaking, he kept nudging Muniamma with his dirty shoe. Muni jerked away, and with a quivering voice she cried, '*Never!* I will never come to you with a smile!'

'Pluck! I like a woman with pluck!' Raj turned and walked away into the darkness.

Krish was stunned, and so was Muni. Silently, they watched Raj lumber up the hill. After long minutes, Krish turned and yelled at his daughter, 'You've done it again. You are always ruining my life.'

Muniamma remained silent and stared nervously at the dried leaves and purple flowers under the jacaranda tree. Her whole body ached, especially her head. The blood along the gash above her eye was beginning to cake.

Krish continued, 'You probably think this is another victory. But listen to me, you are going to marry Raj. I don't know how I'm going to arrange it, but you will marry him.'

Muniamma bit her lip to stop it from trembling.

Krish turned abruptly and headed up the hill after his partner.

Muni slumped down against the rough bark of the huge tree. She pulled her knees up to her chin and hugged her skinny legs, moaning as she rocked back and forth.

The next Muni knew, Sparky was licking her cheek and the entire search party stood around. Everyone was asking questions while Grandmother gently touched Muni's forehead.

'There ... there now, child,' Grandmother was saying. 'God has let us find you.'

'Where was God a minute ago when my father and Raj were here?' Muniamma wanted to scream. But she didn't.

Poonamah quickly took off the warm wool blanket in which she was wrapped, and put it around Muni's shoulders. 'That's better. This blanket will keep you from the shivers. And don't you worry about running away from the baptism.'

Muniamma was touched by her grandmother's love. Old Ma had changed. Once again, she felt surprise at the drastic difference in Grandmother since she had become a Christian. This was just a

'This blanket will keep you from the shivers.'

fleeting thought, and then she screamed, 'I won't marry that horrid man! No one can make me marry him!'

Chapter Four

An hour later, Krish hid in the shadows outside Aunt Sita and Uncle's home. No one suspected he was still lurking about. From where he stood, it was easy to see into their open window. His old mother sat on the sofa next to Muniamma, and Sita sat on Muni's other side.

Others were crowded into the room, but Krish's frown deepened as he noticed the missionary family. They looked concerned, especially the blonde twins and their brother, but Krish was sure they were not sincere. He had never known a close relationship with whites, and a true friendship was more than he could imagine.

He sneaked a little closer to the window to hear the conversation. He noticed his daughter's forehead had been bandaged, her hair combed and dried, and someone had given her a thick blue sweater.

Poonamah patted Muni's hand as they sat close together. Then she looked at Mrs Morton. 'Do you honestly believe my granddaughter will be all right?'

'Yes,' Mary Morton reassured. 'I don't think the cut on her forehead will even leave a scar.'

Grandmother visibly relaxed.

'That is wonderful to hear,' Aunt Sita said as she leaned closer to Muni and Poonamah. 'But don't forget, scars of the heart are harder to heal.'

For a moment they pondered Sita's words. Then Muni began sobbing, and she hiccuped as she cried, 'Father can't make me marry Raj, can he?'

'No child,' Grandmother soothed.

Uncle interrupted, 'Poonamah, we must remember *Krish* is her father.'

Grandmother shook her head, and her double chin swung as she talked. 'I know he's Muniamma's father, but he ran away the day she was born.'

Mr Morton stepped forward and leaned against the edge of the sofa. 'That may be true, but legally he is still her father.'

'Will that make a difference?' Aunt Sita asked.

'Who cares?' Sue shouted. 'No father, legal or not, can make his daughter marry a man against her wishes!'

'Hush, Sue,' Mary Morton admonished. 'You are speaking of things you know nothing about.'

Sue was going to argue with her mother, but Lou poked her in the side. Sue turned, and as she stamped out of the room, her rumpled yellow skirt flew from side to side.

'Excuse our daughter,' Mrs Morton said to their Indian friends. 'Sue is upset about this whole ordeal—as we all are. It's beyond our understanding how a father could treat his own daughter so despicably.'

Grandmother spoke up. 'I don't blame you for being upset. Muniamma's father has always been a mystery. I can honestly say that my son hated his daughter even before she was born. Remember how he put that terrible curse on her from the Hindu goddess Kali? There is something wicked inside him, and he's brought us all much grief.'

For a brief moment, a strange emotion, almost akin to shame, descended upon Krish. He stepped back farther into the shadows. He broke off a small twig from the huge tree he was under and began twisting it round and round. The lines on his dark face became deep crevices.

'He certainly is a strange man,' Mr Morton added. 'I've never met anyone like him or like that partner of his.'

Muniamma gasped, 'Oh Ma! I won't marry that man. I won't!'

'Now...now,' Grandmother said soothingly. 'You've just told us that Raj refuses to marry you unless you come to him willingly and with respect. It seems to me that the problem is solved. There will be no wedding.'

The twig which Krish had been twisting snapped in his hands. He spat, but the spittle stayed on his unshaven chin. 'There will be a wedding,' he vowed under his breath. 'I want Raj's money...I need Raj's money!'

From within the house, Aunt Sita's voice over-lapped Krish's hoarse whisper. 'Listen everyone—'

She paused while thinking how best to say it. 'Remember that old, toothless woman, Mrs Reddy, who was causing such a commotion at the baptismal service today? The one who was screaming and taunting Muni? Well, I think I recognise her. I met her years ago, and if I remember rightly, she has some special powers. If she knew what was happening now, she could devise an evil spell which could make Muniamma fall madly in love with Krish's partner.'

'What?' Mary Morton questioned, her face bewildered. She'd never heard of such happenings in England. 'Are you saying that Mrs Reddy has evil powers at her command and can make Muniamma do things against her own wishes?'

'No!' Kenny said. 'That's just not possible.' He ran his fingers through his straight brown hair.

'How?' Lou added, plopping down on a nearby chair.

'Never!' Muniamma shouted. This was too much.

'Wait a minute,' Mr Morton added. 'We don't have to be afraid. We're on Jesus Christ's side, and victory is ours.'

'That's right,' Uncle added. 'This Mrs Reddy may have evil powers, but we possess the power of the risen Christ.'

'I know,' Aunt Sita responded anxiously. 'I know that, but you don't realise what this old woman can do.'

As the discussion continued, Krish leaned forward to try and catch every word that Aunt Sita said. Just then Mr Naidoo came to his back door.

'Who's out here?' Raneesh's father called.

Krish remained in the shadows.

Mr Naidoo came towards him. 'Hey there, what are you doing?'

'Nothing,' Krish responded. He scuffed at a clump of mud and tossed the twisted twig onto the ground.

'Well, move on. I don't like strangers hanging around my house.'

'Shush,' Krish said angrily, and looked over at the neighbours' open window. He did not want his relatives or the Christians to know he had been standing there, listening.

Mr Naidoo looked at his neighbours' house and then back at Krish. 'I know you,' he whispered. 'You're that girl's father. Come.' He led Krish to his back door. 'I don't blame you for sneaking around.'

Krish didn't say anything. He just wanted this man to go away so he could hear what Aunt Sita was saying about the powers of the old woman.

'That's right,' Mr Naidoo continued and he shook his head as he talked. 'I don't even blame you for being angry. Whoever heard of a Hindu turning to be a Christian? It is the white man's influence, and it's not good. It's destroying our whole way of life.' Mr Naidoo was a tall, handsome Indian man, but tonight his face looked genuinely disturbed.

Krish swore and kicked at the ground again. He knew Mr Naidoo would not go away, so he decided to play along. 'We need to do something. My mother always used to say, "If you were born a Hindu you should die a Hindu."'

For several moments, Mr Naidoo stood silently in the hazy glow from the dim backyard light. The air was still. 'My thoughts exactly,' he said with real feeling. 'And just look, now your old mother has become a Christian, and she's been baptised. And maybe the next time your daughter will have enough nerve to go through with it as well. I believe it's time for action. I've been tolerant long enough, and now even my son, Raneesh, is involved with this Christian group.'

Krish stepped closer. 'What do you plan to do to stop the boy?'

'Well, I'm going to insist that Raneesh stop going to their church meetings. He isn't to be allowed to talk with any Christians.'

'That's a start,' Krish replied, but he was thinking of much more violent means.

'And I am also going to buy a shrine. I saw one a couple of weeks ago for sale. Yes, I'm going to buy it and put it right in front of my home.'

This sounded like an utterly stupid idea to Krish, but he remained silent as Mr Naidoo proceeded.

'Maybe if we become more devout Hindus this kind of adverse influence would have no chance of continuing. Years ago my wife and I were good Hindus, and she would go into trances for people. She had a gift.' Mr Naidoo looked intently at Krish and continued excitedly, 'Maybe it's not too late. All we Hindus need to bind together and preserve our way of life.'

41

Krish had not thought about it. He was so concerned about his selfish motives that he had not considered the broader picture. It wasn't any of his business anyway, he reasoned. All he cared about was getting money for his business venture.

'It's good to see another devout parent,' Mr Naidoo continued. 'Come on into my lounge and sit down. Let's discuss this problem.'

Krish was suspicious, but after more discussion, he slyly suggested, 'There is an old woman in town who may have some good advice for us.'

'Who?'

'You met her earlier today. She was that toothless woman at the baptismal service, the one who was causing such a disturbance.'

'I remember. That's old Mrs Reddy from down the coast. She lives at the sugar mill barracks. I've heard she's come here to Isipingo to say prayers at the temple for some sick relative. Do you think she will help our cause?'

'Yes, I do,' Krish reassured him with a smile. He knew Mr Naidoo did not detect his true motives. All he wanted was to meet the old woman and get her to make Muniamma change her mind about marrying Raj.

It was late when Mr Naidoo offered Krish the bed in his back room. It had been as easy as that. Luck was on his side, Krish reasoned. He could not have been better placed if he had planned it himself! It was absolutely perfect. He was now living right next door to Sita and her husband and could keep an eye on everything. Now he could make new plans which he knew would definitely include more violent means than Mr Naidoo ever thought possible.

Chaper Five

Later, around midnight, Muniamma and Grandmother got into the front of Uncle's truck. Ken was
playfully encouraging Sparky to jump into the back
of the pickup, and the twins, standing by the road-
side, were giggling at their brother's antics.

'Hush now!' Mary Morton admonished. She
held her youngest child, Shelley, in her arms, now
sound asleep. 'It's late, and if you don't settle down
you'll wake up your little sister and all the
neighbours.'

Muniamma looked at the Morton kids. They
didn't seem to have a care in the world. They managed to get Sparky into the truck a little more
quietly, stifling their giggles. Once again,
Muniamma was surprised how quickly they
changed. One minute they were upset, and the next
thing she knew, they were laughing.

'Sue, please take Shelley from your mother and
put her to bed,' Mr Morton said. 'And I want you all
to get to bed right away. Your older sister went to
sleep hours ago.'

'Dad,' Ken said irritably.

'Ken, do as I say. And you too,' he said to the twins before they could respond.

As the Morton kids went inside Aunt Sita and Uncle's home, they grumbled. For a brief moment, Muniamma wished she could join them, but then she thought, *No, I want to go home. I want to be far away from Father and his awful partner—and especially from old Mrs Reddy.* Muniamma swallowed hard to try and keep down her fear as she recalled Aunt Sita's words explaining Mrs Reddy's extraordinary powers. She longed to be up in their little shack in the hills above Isipingo. 'Let's go, Ma.'

'Just a minute,' Poonamah said. 'Sita is telling me about a plan for next Sunday.'

Aunt Sita held onto the door of the truck by Grandmother's side. She smiled at Muni and then addressed Poonamah. 'Listen, there are some new Christians I've heard about who live further down the coast at the sugar mill. Pastor Moonsami is working there, and he and his wife live in the barracks along with the other mill workers. Why don't we all go down there next Sunday to encourage them?'

Ma nodded thoughtfully.

'Your reputation as a public Hindu has been well known, Poonamah. It will encourage this group to hear that you have become a Christian. They've been praying for you and Muniamma for a long time. And you can tell them about this new development with Krish and his partner and have them pray with you.'

Ma nodded again.

What business do we have going anywhere? Muniamma thought. *Don't we have enough problems of our own?* She wanted to stay up in the hills away from her father and Raj.

Finally Grandmother answered with deep resolve, 'We'll go.'

'Good,' Aunt Sita said and shut the truck door. 'We'll see you next week.'

As they pulled away from the kerb, Muni looked over at Raneesh's home. The lights were out, and all seemed quiet. *I wonder if Raneesh will come with us next Sunday?* she thought, and then chided herself. *We have so many problems of our own. Why should we be travelling around encouraging others?*

They were on the outskirts of town when Grandmother looked past Muni and addressed Uncle. 'That was a good idea of Sita's. Muniamma and I will both go with you; it will be a privilege. We will walk to your house early next Sunday morning.'

'I'll come and pick you up.'

'No. We'll walk. Besides, you'll have plenty to do to get ready for the trip.'

Poonamah and Uncle continued making plans while Muniamma listened with mixed emotions. It all sounded rather exciting, but Muni had a sneaking suspicion all would not go as planned. Somehow something would happen to spoil it.

As the truck left town and headed up the small rutted road through the sugar cane, Muniamma quickly glanced from one side of the road to the other. Anyone could be hiding in the tall cane, her

46

father, or Raj, or even old Mrs Reddy.

Muniamma shivered.

'Relax,' Uncle said. 'You're all tense and nervous. Everything will work out. Don't keep worrying about your father or his partner. You'll see, God will have a way to deal with them.'

Muniamma held her breath and stared down at her clenched fists.

'Uncle's right,' Grandmother agreed. 'We'll be home soon, and I'm sure you will feel better after a good night's sleep. And don't give a second thought to what Sita said about that old toothless woman we saw today. Krish doesn't even know her. You are no concern of Mrs Reddy's, and she'll put no evil spell on you.'

Muniamma shivered again and pulled the thick sweater tighter around her bony shoulders.

Ma looked out of the cracked window of the truck and continued talking. She was not addressing anyone in particular, but seemed to be thinking out loud. 'It has been a long day. We walked down this path this morning, and so much has happened since then.'

No one said a word. Words were unnecessary. They all knew what had happened; they had been there. Muniamma felt especially embarrassed remembering how she had run away from the baptismal service. And then she recalled painfully every horrid detail surrounding her encounter at the cemetery with her father and that awful Raj. Nervously she touched the bandage above her left eye.

There was silence all the rest of the way until Uncle slowed to a stop. He came as near as he could to their small shack. Sparky jumped out from the back of the truck and dashed up to the banana grove where his bowl was kept.

'Take care,' Uncle yelled above the sputtering of the engine. Then Uncle noticed the pile of burned wood where Ma's Hindu shrine used to stand. He chuckled, 'You really did destroy your shrine, didn't you?'

Ma nodded and smiled.

Muniamma watched as Uncle drove away. The headlights illuminated the sugar cane as he descended the hill, and Muni shivered again. Quickly she turned and ran into their house. Ma lit the kerosene lantern, and Muni pulled the thin curtains. Shadows flickered across the cement-plastered walls and corrugated tin roofing.

Muni needed to use the outdoor toilet, but she did not want to go alone. Soon they were both crowded into the single bed and the lamp was turned off. It wasn't long before Ma started snoring. Muniamma turned over onto her side, away from Grandmother, and stared around their one-room home. The reflection from the moon was not very bright, and dark shadows seemed to be darting everywhere. She pulled the thin blanket over her head and wriggled down further into the crowded bed.

I'll never sleep tonight, she thought. But she was wrong. Immediately she drifted into a much-needed sleep. Tomorrow and the next day and the following week would come with problems of their own. Tonight, however, Muniamma slept.

Chapter Six

Every day, in their shack in the hills, Muniamma read from her Bible to Grandmother. Their early morning times meant increasingly more to them. Neither of them had ever heard the creation story and were fascinated by how the serpent deceived Eve.

'Ma, isn't it strange how it was a serpent that tricked the first woman? Remember how Aunt Sita used to worship the Hindu snake goddess before she became a Christian?'

'I remember, child. Read on.'

Conversations constantly interrupted their reading, but neither granddaughter nor grandmother minded, for they were becoming inseparable. They cried. They laughed. They prayed. They understood. It was as if a protective hedge had been lovingly placed around their home and garden. The week was ideal. It was like entering a beautiful calm harbour after spending a terrifying night out in the midst of a stormy sea.

Muniamma's nervousness began gradually to ease. Even the hours spent working in Madame Van

Conversations constantly interrupted their reading...

Niekerk's garden became a healing balm. In fact, there were times when Muni almost forgot about her father, Raj, and even Mrs Reddy. Almost, but not completely.

When Aunt Sita and Uncle came for a visit towards the end of the week, they were astonished at the obvious changes and even commented about the calm understanding which had developed between the two.

Early the following Sunday, before dawn, Grandmother and Muniamma prepared to leave for their trip into Isipingo for church and then to the sugar mill barracks. It was decided that Sparky would have to stay, so Muniamma reluctantly tied him to the thick stalks of the banana bushes in the grove close to their home. His rope was long, allowing him plenty of room to run back and forth in the shade. Muni filled his bowls with food and water and knelt down to say goodbye.

'I'll see you tonight, Sparky. It's going to be late. But you be good, do you hear?' Muni rubbed him lovingly behind his big floppy ears. Sparky licked her face, and she giggled, 'Oh, you're so precious! I wish you could come with us, but Ma says you would get in the way at the barracks. You're probably better off here in the shade.' Muni hugged him again before she turned to go. 'Now, take care of the place for us, all right?'

Sparky barked as Muniamma and Poonamah began their two-hour walk into town. For quite some distance they could hear him yelping. Muni felt sad because she knew her dog hated to be tied up.

Poonamah had killed one of their old chickens the previous day and had even plucked it. This was to be a gift to the new Christians at the sugar mill barracks and would help with the curry dinner they would most likely insist on preparing. Ma held the scrawny fowl by its feet, and the broken neck flopped back and forth with each step.

The sugar cane smelled sweet, and Muni broke off a piece and began chewing. The top of the cane was green, and the rolling hills, which stretched out for miles before them, looked like a velvet green carpet. But as they turned and headed down the firebreaker line, Muniamma looked at the old brown stalks of the cane on either side of the path. It did not look so green and lush up close, but brown and dirty. Large cane rats could even be heard scurrying around.

'When are the Van Niekerks going to burn the cane?' Muni asked.

'Oh, not for at least another month. The mill is still shut for repairs. The people who own the mill do this every year and during these few months no farmer burns his fields. Besides, this section of cane is not ready for burning.'

Muniamma knew that the Van Niekerks always set their fields alight by controlled burns when the cane was ready for harvest. That was the reason they had hacked out firebreaker lines. The controlled fire would burn the green on top of the cane and most of the rubble around the ground, leaving the stems, which contained the sugar, exposed. This burning made the harvesting easier.

The previous year, Muni had seen the whole fascinating process. The sky lit up with the burning and the thick black smoke smelled sweet. Muniamma had something to look forward to. She also enjoyed watching the Africans cut off the burned stalks by hand and seeing the huge metal cranes as they picked up and loaded one-ton bundles into the back of the old cane trucks. Yes, some exciting times were ahead.

'Ma, what would happen if this field caught fire now?' Muniamma was recalling how irate Mr Van Niekerk had been just a week and a half ago over the bonfire she and Ma had started when they burned their Hindu shrine.

'If this field were to burn now, it would probably mean ruin for the Van Niekerks. With the mills shut, the burned stalks would remain here and rot.'

Muniamma felt awful. 'No wonder Mr Van Niekerk was so angry with us when we set fire to our shrine.'

Ma shook her head. 'He had reason to be mad.'

They kept walking on and on. Eventually they watched in awe as the sun finally peeked above the horizon, stretching red fingers of brilliant light across the blue of the Indian Ocean and then up over the town of Isipingo, and finally right into the lush green hills where they walked. Muniamma had always enjoyed the sunrise, but now it held infinitely more meaning because she was beginning to know and love the God of the sunrise.

Muniamma wondered if Grandmother was experiencing similar thoughts and was going to say something as she turned and looked at her. But Ma's rapt expression said it all, so Muniamma remained silent and continued watching breathlessly as the red sky turned vivid pink and finally a soft blue. By this time they were almost into town. Their walk and the resulting thoughts had become a time of worship and adoration to the God of creation. Now they felt ready for the day.

As they walked through town the few people they saw seemed to be whispering and pointing in their direction. Her heart beat faster, and all the time she kept wishing they had stayed in the hills, hidden and protected. She felt certain her father would appear at any time and hurl threats and abuse.

When they came to Aunt and Uncle's street they noticed more commotion than usual, although the activity was not centred only around Aunt and Uncle's home, but Raneesh's. The shape of his house looked odd. A small room had been added which extended directly from the front door. In fact, one now had to walk through this small room to enter Raneesh's house. Mr Naidoo, Raneesh's father, stood by the entrance, from which were strung several multi-coloured plastic garlands. Muniamma immediately noticed that even Mr Naidoo looked different. He wore a garland around his neck and had an ash thumbprint in the middle of his forehead. He was talking to a man and woman, encouraging them to enter the little room.

'What's this, Ma? What's going on?'

Poonamah sadly shook her head. 'It seems Mr Naidoo has built a small Hindu temple, or he's bought one and attached it to his home. It looks an awful lot like one of those old one-room prayer stalls that stood on the grounds, next to the fire-pit, near the temple.'

'What's he doing?'

'Well, that's hard to say. To my way of thinking, he's just plain scared because of what he saw last Sunday right here in his front yard and down by the sea, where I was baptised. But I'm sure others would disagree with me and say only that Mr Naidoo has become a more devout Hindu because he has set up a service to the Hindu neighbours.'

'What? I still don't understand what's happening.' Muniamma wanted to ask if Ma thought Raneesh was all right, but felt it was not wise. Grandmother might not understand.

'Come, child. Stop your staring and let's hurry into Aunt and Uncle's home. They have the church service to get ready for and then the trip immediately after. I'm sure there are ways we can help.'

Muniamma did not want to help. How could Grandmother think of moving furniture around in preparation for the church service and packing up food for the trip? But she obediently followed, all the same.

When they entered, they saw that a few of the church people had already arrived and had the room ready for the service. Muniamma could hear giggling in the kitchen—the Morton twins. She took the dead fowl from Grandmother, 'I'll take this into the kitchen for you, OK?'

'Good morning, Muniamma,' Sue greeted, as soon as Muni entered the kitchen. 'Oh horrors! Look at that skinny chicken!' Sue exclaimed and giggled again.

Muniamma put the ugly thing behind her back and stammered a few awkward words.

Sue looked genuinely contrite. 'I'm sorry. I didn't mean to embarrass you or anything. I was just trying to be funny.'

Lou came over and extended her hand. 'Here, let me take this and put it in the refrigerator. And why don't you come and help us make some salads for the dinner this afternoon?'

Muni handed the offending creature to Lou and went over to the table where Sue stood.

'Hey, I think that gash on your forehead is healing nicely,' Sue said, trying hard to make up for her blunder.

Muniamma smiled.

'We're going with you today to the sugar mill,' Sue added excitedly. 'This week in school we were studying about how sugar is processed. Do you think we'll get a tour through the mill?'

'I...er...don't know.'

'The teacher told us that it's shut down right now for repairs but maybe, if we're lucky, we'll still be able to go inside and see the machines and everything.'

'We're not going there to learn about sugar,' Lou scolded her sister. 'We're going to visit some new Christians.' Lou turned to Muni and handed her some beetroot to grate for the salad.

'Our whole family was so excited when we were invited to come along,' Sue interjected, as if she hadn't heard her sister's rebuke. 'This trip is really going to be super.' Then Sue turned and made a face at her sister. 'And I'm still hoping that even if the mill is having some repairs done, somebody will still let us see inside.'

Muniamma picked up a beetroot and began grating it. There was silence in the kitchen for some time, and then Muniamma finally mustered up enough courage to ask, 'What's going on next door? Have either of you seen Raneesh?'

Sue and Lou exchanged glances. 'Well,' Lou explained, 'we moved into our own house this week, so we haven't been here very much. We have seen Raneesh a couple of times, but we weren't allowed to talk to him.'

'Not allowed?'

'That's right. His parents refuse to let him talk with any of us Christians and he's definitely not allowed to come to church any more. Mr Naidoo bought a small temple and he's set it up at the front of their house. We've heard that Raneesh's mother is going into trances, and she's telling people's fortunes and all sorts of things.'

Muniamma kept grating and pieces of beetroot flew everywhere.

'And there's more,' Sue added.

'More?' Muni could hardly believe it. She desperately longed to be back with Sparky in the hills.

The twins exchanged glances again, then Lou continued, 'We've heard that your father has moved in next door, also that old woman, Mrs Reddy, is hanging around an awful lot.'

Muniamma plopped down on the chair and buried her face in her hands. Drops of beetroot juice got into her hair and dripped onto her faded dress, leaving little purple smears.

'It's not the end of the world!' Sue exclaimed. 'Honestly Muniamma, it's not as bad as all that. Something will happen and everything will turn around and get better. That old woman can't put any spell on you which will make you want to get married.'

'That's right,' Lou added. 'We've been praying about this all week. You're safe, I'm sure of it.'

Muniamma wished desperately that she felt the same, but the thought still plagued her: *Where was God when she was knocked down under the jacaranda tree? Why hadn't he allowed her to escape and never meet that awful Raj?* Muniamma's hand shook as

59

she lightly touched the wound above her left eye. It was beginning to heal. *Why? Why so many problems?* she thought.

Chapter Seven

The morning church service was about to end and Muniamma realised she had not listened to one word. She had not paid attention even to the songs that Mr Singh led. Her mind was filled with the news of her father and Mrs Reddy. *Ma and I should have stayed in the hills*, she told herself over and over.

Muniamma was sitting cross-legged on the floor in the front of the room, between Sue and Lou. Leaning forward, she placed her elbows on her knees and her chin on her clasped hands. The strong smell of chillies was still on her fingers because she had cut two large green ones to add to the salad just before the service started. Her eyes smarted from the smell, but it was good because that odour kept bringing her back to the reality of the moment. Every time her mind drifted to her father or to fears of what was about to happen, that strong smell of the green chillies brought her straight back to the present.

The smarting in her eyes also reminded her of how her eyes had burned and swollen shut after her terrible bout with the measles not too many weeks earlier. The Christian God had healed her eyes; she knew for certain that he alone had saved her from going blind. She knew that truth ought to have helped her grow more dependent upon the living God, but she was too preoccupied with her earthly father and his plans.

Mr Singh was closing the service with a prayer, asking God to go before the families who were about to visit the new Christians down the coast at the sugar mill barracks.

Muniamma breathed deeply and tried to concentrate on being less tense. *God will have to use someone else to encourage those people,* she reasoned to herself, *because I feel totally incapable of helping anyone.*

The service finally ended and her friend Vijay came forward to greet her. Muni quickly looked at Vijay's skin to see if the red, oozing sores were actually gone. Vijay noticed Muniamma's quick look and laughed. 'Yes, I'm still healed. See, take a look at my legs where the sores were the worst.' Vijay stuck out one leg so Muni could see it better. 'When God heals you, he does it completely.'

Muniamma felt embarrassed. Had her look been so obvious?

'My mother and I will be praying for you as you leave today,' Vijay promised with her soft, gentle voice. 'It is wonderful that you and your grandmother are going to the barracks to encourage others. I'm sure that as you look after those new Christians and listen to them, you too will be healed from all your hurts.'

Muniamma stared at Vijay. 'What do you mean?'

'I'm sorry. I didn't mean to be bold or anything,

Vijay stuck out one leg so Muni could see it better.

but I've been watching you this morning during church. You look really troubled and...er...I wanted to encourage you with the thought that helping others sometimes helps us the most.'

She knew exactly what Vijay was trying to say. Muniamma wanted to thank her, but did not know how.

There was an awkward silence, then Vijay said, 'You'd better hurry. It looks like those who are going are about to leave. I will be praying for you today.'

Muniamma felt reluctant to walk away because she liked the way she talked and felt somehow that Vijay understood. But just then Mrs Morton came and interrupted them.

'Excuse me, girls. Muniamma, would you and the twins please go into the back of Uncle's truck? We'll put the pots of food in the back with you so you can watch them and make sure nothing tips over.'

'Yes, ma'am,' Muniamma answered. 'Can Vijay and her mother come with us to the sugar mill barracks?'

'Oh, we hadn't thought about them. I don't know if there is enough room.'

'It's all right,' Vijay responded. 'We couldn't go at such short notice.'

'Well, maybe next time,' the missionary said kindly. 'Now please hurry Muniamma, we're a bit late.'

No one suspected that old Mrs Reddy was lurking in the shade nearby. She had overheard every word. But she was especially interested in the comments about the barracks—her home. Why were these Christians going to the sugar mill? What business did they have down there? Instantly she was alert and angry.

'Yes, ma'am,' Muni was saying to the missionary. 'I'll be glad to sit in the truck and hold the food.'

As Mary Morton walked away, Muni turned to Vijay, 'I wish you were coming.'

'Maybe next time,' Vijay smiled and then held Muni's hands for a brief moment. 'You go and have a good time and forget about your problems. You and your grandmother have a lot to say about becoming Christians.'

Not once had Vijay mentioned Muni's father or Raj when referring to Muniamma's problem, nor had she referred to Mrs Reddy and her powers. She hadn't even mentioned Muniamma's running away from the baptismal service last Sunday. This showed deep respect, and Muni felt grateful. She smiled.

Muniamma would not have smiled, however, if she had seen the look which descended upon old Mrs Reddy's wrinkled face as she continued listening to their conversation.

Vijay's encouraging words brought some comfort to Muniamma as she got into the back of the pickup and arranged the pots of food and bowls of salad so that nothing would spill. She looked over at Raneesh's home. All she could see was Mr Naidoo inside his small temple with two others. Muni noticed that prayer lamps were lit in front of several Hindu images that were arranged on narrow shelves. Raneesh was nowhere in sight, and neither was Krish nor his partner...nor the old, toothless woman. In spite of the warm day, Muniamma shivered as the truck pulled out to follow Pastor Morton and his family in their van.

The trip down the coast was pleasant. Along with the twins, she loved the feel of the wind rushing through her hair. Every so often they spotted small, make-shift stalls along the edge of the road, where African women displayed their home-made items. The black women waved vigorously at the traffic to try and encourage people to stop and shop.

Though the truck was travelling fast, Muniamma could still see scores of clay pots, grass mats, crocheted blankets and hundreds of handwoven baskets on display by the Bantu women. She wanted to stop and admire their work, but Pastor Morton kept on driving with Uncle following. Muniamma also saw tables overloaded with colourful souvenirs and trinkets. She could not distinguish what they were because they passed too quickly.

The rough sea was on their left, visible from the road most of the time. Muni took deep breaths and tried to relax. It was beginning to work. Just being away from Isipingo brought comfort. And watching the scenery of avocado and pawpaw trees and huge palm trees flash by brought a refreshing change. Muniamma consciously tried to forget her problems and concentrate on the beauty around her.

Finally they turned off the road that ran parallel to the Indian Ocean and headed inland. Before long they came to the town that had been built around the sugar mill. As they passed the gates to the town, one of the first things Muniamma noticed was a Hindu temple on one side of the dirt road and a small Christian church on the other. It was unusually hot and dry for this time of year, and dust swirled around their heads.

Pastor Morton pulled over and came to a stop. He yelled out of his car window to a group of Indian boys who were playing cricket in the street. 'Hey, could one of you please tell me where Pastor Moonsami lives? He is the pastor of this church.' The missionary pointed to the little white building with the words 'JESUS SAVES' printed in blue paint above the door. The windows of the church were open, and Muni could see inside. There were a few scattered songbooks on the benches, and in front a vase was filled with bright orange flowers.

After receiving polite, detailed directions, they thanked the helpful youths and started down the narrow streets of the town. The barracks were all arranged in long, even rows, and every street they came to looked exactly like the last.

Eventually, after jolting through the ruts, they stopped behind one of the barracks. Muniamma noticed a pack of dogs rummaging through a rubbish heap. The dogs stopped just long enough to growl and bare their teeth at the intruders before they went back to their frantic search for food. She was thankful Sparky had stayed at home.

The parade of visitors got out and began to walk, carrying their pots of food. The barracks looked strange because about four houses were connected, and down one side were the entrances to each of these homes. Then across a narrow cement walkway, facing the entrance to the homes, were two kitchen areas. This meant that two households shared one kitchen, but each family had its own sitting room and two bedrooms.

People stuck their heads out of the doors as the newcomers walked past and across to the next row of barracks. Women stopped their cooking in the small open kitchens and stared at the visitors. Two monkeys scurried up the trunk of a nearby tree and this scared little Shelley. Her screams brought even more attention.

Maybe Poonamah and Muni or even Aunt Sita and Uncle by themselves would not have attracted so many stares, but the Mortons were different. Some of the Indian women looked resentful about having a white family present, though others smiled and greeted them politely.

As they neared the home of Pastor Moonsami, a sickening, putrid odour made Muni wrinkle her face in disgust; and they soon discovered that the minister's house was located close to the communal toilets. The stench made Mary Morton wonder if she should have brought Shelley, and Sue and Lou began to whisper complaints. Their older sister, Kathie, hushed them and with a grown-up expression reminded the twins to look around at the people and forget the surroundings. All the same, Muniamma noticed that Kathie tiptoed carefully in her light beige canvas sandals. She also noticed Kathie's nose, wrinkled up like her own as she looked down at her new shoes and dusted them twice before they came to Pastor Moonsami's home.

Soon the procession arrived, and the first thing they saw was a wooden cross hanging on his heavy aluminium front door. It was unmistakable and distinct, especially as most of the other homes had plastic garlands or strings of lime leaves strung above the doorways—a common practice for Hindus.

Uncle knocked softly and stood back. Immediately, Pastor Moonsami came out. His surprise was genuine. 'Oh, praise be to God! What an answer to prayer. Come. Come on into my humble home and sit down. What a pleasure!' Pastor Moonsami was short and plump and he still had on his three-piece suit from the Sunday morning service.

All the visitors crowded into the Moonsami home. There were not enough chairs for everyone, so Muni stood in the narrow hallway with Ken and the twins. Pastor Moonsami quickly went outside and shouted, 'Indra, come. We have visitors.'

He stuck his head back into the room and explained, 'My wife is in the kitchen across the walkway. She will come and make you a cool drink.'

Then, with a quizzical expression, the Indian pastor looked at Poonamah and then over at Muni. 'Aren't you the ones I met at Uncle and Aunt Sita's around Easter time?'

'Yes,' Ma agreed and smiled. 'And I'm the one who marched out of that church meeting and took my granddaughter with me.'

The minister looked at Uncle in surprise.

'That's right. But God has done a real work in their lives since then. In fact, last Sunday, Poonamah went through the waters of baptism.'

Muniamma stared at the worn pattern on the linoleum floor. She hoped Uncle would not mention that she had run away and hidden in the graveyard instead of being baptised.

Uncle continued, 'We are here to tell you all about Poonamah's and Muniamma's conversion. We want to share this news with other new Christians in this area and pray together.'

'Praise the Lord!' the Indian pastor and his wife, Indra, exclaimed together. Indra had just entered with their four-year-old son, who clung to her side and hid his face in the fullness of her sari.

'Welcome. Please, please make yourselves comfortable,' the beautiful Indian lady said. 'I'll prepare something to drink. Then we can sit and enjoy one another while we wait for the curry to finish cooking.'

Aunt Sita rose. 'Let us help. We've brought along plenty of food, as you can see.' And she pointed to the large pots which Kathie, Ken, Muniamma and the twins held and to the skinny dead fowl in Grandmother's grasp.

'Oh ... you shouldn't have,' Indra protested. But it was obvious she was extremely pleased.

Pastor Moonsami smiled. 'You ladies go and finish preparing the meal and Uncle, Mr Morton and I will invite the two new Christian families to come and join us.'

All the adults carried the pots into the kitchen and even Kathie left with the women to work in the open shelter. Big tanks of propane stood to one side and hoses ran from these to burners on which the pots of food rested. Soon the smell of curry filled the air, and Muniamma's stomach growled.

Sue giggled. 'I'm hungry too. Isn't this place the limit? Where are we all going to eat? Everything's so crowded.'

'I don't know,' Ken said. 'But I'm going with the men. I want to see more of these barracks and maybe even meet some of those cricket players.'

The girls walked to the door with Ken, and as they looked out Mrs Morton met them. 'Take care of Shelley, will you? She's clinging onto me so much that I'm getting worn out, but I don't want her around those propane burners. And why don't you girls also watch Indra's little boy?'

'Sure, Mum,' Lou answered. 'Isn't this wonderful? I'm so glad we're here. Isn't this place just fascinating?'

'Yes, Lou, it is. And I'm thankful we're here, too. Now, girls, watch these little children for me and be careful not to wander too far away. And don't take Shelley near those toilets. Who knows what diseases are around here.'

Mary Morton stopped and smiled at the astonished expressions on all three of the young teen faces. 'Well, if Shelley needs to go, let her, but be careful, all right?'

'Yes, ma'am,' Muniamma said. She was proud to have such an important task.

Sue giggled at her mother's anxiety and squeamishness. 'We'll be careful. Mum, do you think we'll be able to go through the mill and see how sugar is made?'

'Perhaps. We'll see.'

This was proving to be an interesting day.

Chapter Eight

It was more than an interesting day for Krish, who remained behind in Isipingo. He was still staying at Raneesh's home and was comfortably occupying a small back bedroom.

'Finally, luck is with me,' he said as he picked up his beer can and peered out of the window. The Christians were coming out of Uncle and Aunt Sita's home after the church service. Their obvious joy made his thin, dark face turn darker.

He noticed his skinny daughter getting into the back of the pickup with the blonde twins. Pots of food were carefully placed with them, and the sight of them made Krish boil with anger.

'What do they think they're doing?' he asked under his breath. He spoke to no one in particular; he was alone. 'It looks like they're going on a stupid picnic!'

When he saw his old mother proudly carrying a plucked fowl, Krish's hand began to shake in rage. Beer sloshed out of the can and onto the sheer curtains. Quickly he downed his drink and crushed the tin. 'Enough! Today's the day for action. I'm tired of sitting around, waiting for something to happen. I'll make it happen!'

Krish thought back over his week at the Naidoos'. Numerous times he had tried to talk Raj into changing his mind and agree to marry Muniamma regardless of how she felt. However, Raj was sticking to his proud plan; he wanted Muniamma only if she became a willing bride.

Krish kicked the beer can. He had to do something quickly. He wanted Raj's money.

For a moment, Krish stopped and contemplated Mr and Mrs Naidoo's method of coping with their problems. They had been true to Mr Naidoo's word and had conscientiously gone back to their Hindu religion. Krish was sick of their repetitious prayers to the many gods and goddesses. He did not believe in the Hindu way and was tired of the crowds coming in and out of the shrine which had been erected in front of the Naidoo home.

'What utter fools,' he sputtered.

To Krish's way of thinking, though, one encouraging thing had occurred during the long week; the shrine had brought old Mrs Reddy. She had come many times, but as yet Krish had not had a chance to talk with her. He wasn't even sure she had special powers as Sita had claimed. In some ways she seemed just an old fool to him, and yet....

When Krish looked out of the window again, Uncle's truck was pulling away from the kerb. Krish pulled the curtain back to get a better look. Immediately, he spotted Mrs Reddy hiding behind a tree. She was standing very still, and her back was straighter than he had ever seen it. Her stance looked rigid. 'I wonder what the old biddy's doing?' he laughed.

He was about to let the curtain drop when the old woman turned around. Krish gasped. He couldn't believe his own eyes. Absolute shock filled his body, turning his limbs weak. He stared in disbelief at the grotesque expression which stretched across the old hag's face. Her thin lips were pulled hideously away from her darkened gums, and her toothless grimace sent violent chills up and down Krish's spine. The whites of Mrs Reddy's eyes turned yellow, and her pupils became like piercing red pinpricks.

Krish swung away from the window and fell against the wall. Very little disturbed him, but for once he felt shaken to the bone. He desperately hoped that the old woman hadn't seen him stare.

'Maybe Sita was right after all,' he whispered hoarsely. 'Maybe old Mrs Reddy does have some extraordinary powers.'

Gradually Krish's panicky breathing began to ease. Questions filled his mind: why is the old woman so upset? What could have infuriated her? Whom is she angry with? Finally, he whispered through clenched teeth, 'I've got to talk to her today while she's still mad. We have to work together. I need her to concoct a spell to make Muniamma marry Raj.'

Krish cautiously went back to the window and peeped out. The woman was nowhere in sight.

Just then there was a knock on his door. 'Go

away,' he yelled. He felt certain it was Raneesh, and Krish was sick of that boy. He knew that if he saw Raneesh again this morning he would hit him. The boy had even dared to say that he was praying to the Christian God—praying for Krish and his partner.

Krish picked up the crushed can and threw it at the closed door, cursing loudly.

The door opened and Mrs Reddy herself stood there, silently. She grinned, and once again her thin lips curled back into a sinister snarl.

But it was the evil glare in her eyes that made every nerve in Krish's body tense. He stammered, 'C... c... come on in.'

Mrs Reddy slowly and deliberately closed the door. She walked over to the dresser and looked down at the messy array of Krish's few belongings. Then she walked over to the unmade bed and flicked the sheets. This irritated Krish. When she finally turned and faced him, Krish instantly detected that her expression had changed. She did not look at all menacing; once again she appeared to be just a stupid old woman.

Maybe I was mistaken, Krish thought. *Maybe she doesn't possess any special powers.* This thought made him speak roughly. 'What do you want?'

'Your mother and daughter are Christians.' It was a statement, but it sounded suspiciously like an accusation.

'I know.'

Mrs Reddy continued staring and her words were spoken in a monotone. 'Did you know they are spreading this rubbish? They've just left for the sugar mill barracks.'

'I wondered where they were going.'

'Stop them!'

To be honest, Krish really didn't care what they or anyone else believed; Christian or Hindu, it made no difference to him. Sometimes he made a fuss, but in reality it wasn't all that important to his way of thinking. All Krish wanted was to make his daughter marry Raj so he could get the money he needed for his new business venture.

'I've been wondering if you would concoct a spell for me,' Krish blurted out. 'I'll pay well. I want my daughter to fall in love with a certain man and become a willing bride. I've heard you have extraordinary powers and can cast spells. Will you do it?'

Mrs Reddy turned away and once again looked at the unmade bed and clothes strewn around the room. She did not look at Krish as she spoke. 'Where did you hear I possess such powers?' Her words were whispered.

Krish debated if he had heard correctly.

'Where?' Mrs Reddy repeated, and she turned and looked at Krish. Her toothless mouth appeared ugly, but not one bit as frightening as he had remembered.

Again Krish was surprised and encouraged by the apparent transformation in the old woman. He felt certain he had misinterpreted her earlier expression when she had stood outside under the tree and when she had first entered his room. Shaking his head, he thought of how silly he had been in letting his imagination get out of control.

'Oh, I just heard it around,' he said, and mumbled a few oaths under his breath. Krish was beginning to get back his usual confidence. 'Well, can you do it? Can you put a spell on someone and make her fall madly in love?'

Mrs Reddy did not answer. She began pacing the room. The more she walked around, the more irritable Krish became. He was ready to hurl some vile words at her when the old woman stopped.

'I'm not interested in who your daughter marries. It's no concern of mine. But I do want to stop these Christians. They have no business at the sugar mill barracks. Where does your old mother live?'

The question took Krish by surprise, and he answered quickly, 'She lives up in a shack in the hills. Both she and my daughter, Muniamma, work for some white folks—the Van Niekerks.'

The old woman cackled. 'Good, that's where we'll begin.'

With their heads together, they started discussing the old woman's plan. It was not entirely what Krish had wanted, but it would do for a start.

Chapter Nine

Meanwhile, Muniamma was beginning to relax. Everything at the barracks was so different from what she was used to, and the ride down the coast had helped. She realised, with a growing sense of amazement, that she was enjoying herself. Even the news about her father moving into Raneesh's home was not quite as disturbing as before. She took a deep breath and smiled at the twins. They giggled.

'Let's explore,' Sue said. 'It's just like we're back in the dark ages or something.'

'But we've got to watch Shelley and this little fellow,' Lou reminded her sister. She held both children by the hand.

'That's OK, they can come with us.' Sue crouched down next to Pastor Moonsami's four-year-old son, Deven. 'Sweetie, why don't we go for a walk?'

He began crying, and the more the twins tried to comfort him the more distressed he became.

'Enough of this,' Muniamma interrupted. She picked up the boy and held him in her arms. 'You're being naughty, Deven. Now stop this crying, do you hear? No more.'

To the twins' astonishment, the Indian boy settled down, and Muniamma moved him around to her hip and held him firmly. 'Let's go,' she said to Sue, and the twins giggled again.

'You're a natural mother,' Lou said, and there was real admiration in her tone.

As the three young girls and their two small charges started off down the narrow walkway, Aunt Sita leaned out of the open kitchen, 'Don't go anywhere. We're about to eat. In fact, here is soap and water. I want you all to wash and make sure Shelley's and Deven's hands are clean. And, Muniamma, the men will be returning just now with the guests. I want you to make sure everyone gets the chance to wash before they eat.'

'Yes, Auntie Sita,' Muniamma responded quickly. She took Deven to the chipped enamel basin and washed his hands.

'Don't they have running water?' Sue whispered to Muni.

'No. Not like at Auntie Sita's house where water comes right into the kitchen. But I see a tap,' and Muniamma pointed to a large tap at the far end of the row of barracks. 'I'm sure that water is for all these families to use.'

'No running water! No electricity! How do people live this way?' It was more of a statement than a question.

'Sue!' Lou sounded horrified at her sister's insensitivity. 'That's an awful thing to say. You know Muniamma and her grandmother don't have these things either.'

'Oh, I'm sorry,' Sue pleaded. 'I wasn't thinking, Muni. I wasn't trying to be mean. Honestly!'

'I know,' Muniamma said shyly. 'That's all right. I know you weren't. I guess I've always just been thankful that I don't have to go to a river and carry water like a lot of people do. And I've never lived in a house with electricity. I don't think I'd like it anyhow. The soft glow from a lantern can be so pretty.'

Sue looked embarrassed. 'Sometimes I get so used to all I have that I guess I take it for granted.'

Just then the men returned with the two new Christian families, and everyone was introduced. There was so much commotion that Muniamma leaned back against the side of the house with Deven in her arms.

Aunt Sita nodded meaningfully to Muni and then over at the basin of water. Muniamma obediently put down the small boy and did as she was bidden. She placed the bar of soap in the cold water and the clean towel over her arm. She carried the basin to Pastor Moonsami, who began to wash quickly. He smiled at Muni for her thoughtfulness and said, 'What a lovely girl. Come, guests, please have a wash before you eat. Muniamma will help you.'

Several times Muni had to throw out the water and go back to the tap for more. Finally, all had washed and Pastor Moonsami gathered everyone together for a prayer. Muni was impressed. They stood in a circle outside, by the kitchen, and all held hands while the Indian pastor prayed a simple prayer of thanksgiving to God for friends and food.

The men were served first, and they proceeded into the Moonsami home to sit in the lounge. Then the women made sure all the children had their curry, and finally the ladies dished up their own and remained in the kitchen to eat and talk.

The young people began congregating in the shade of a nearby tree. Ken was already seated on the ground with two boys of nine and twelve, who belonged to the families of the new Christians. Kathie sat near an Indian girl who looked as if she were at least seventeen. Muniamma and the twins went to join them.

As usual, Muniamma ate with her fingers; she looked around at the Mortons, and all of them were eating with their fingers, too. She noticed they were much neater than when they had first tried to eat like the Indians. In fact, they now looked natural, and Muni felt proud of them.

Ken was so engrossed in his conversation with the Indian boys that he looked almost animated. Even the twins and Kathie seemed to hang onto every word the boys were saying, and sometimes their seventeen-year-old sister, Vino, would add a few comments. Muniamma tried to listen, but she could not summon any interest in what they were saying. Instead, she felt an urgency to get up and walk around the barracks. Now she wished she had Sparky with her after all. He would have gladly stayed by her side and gone with her.

When everyone went back for seconds, Muniamma decided to slip away. She wanted the twins to come but, once again, she felt a compulsion to leave immediately so did not even take the time to ask them to join her. Besides, Sue and Lou looked completely enthralled with their new acquaintances, and she knew they would probably not want to leave.

Muniamma wandered down the narrow walkway and skirted the communal toilets. Though she screwed up her nose again in revulsion, she kept on, as if driven, passing row after long row of barracks. She thought of her home up in the Isipingo hills. 'It's so small and isolated,' she thought, 'but I like it. I really don't think I would care to live this close to so many people. The only good thing about living in town would be that I could go to school.'

Once again that inner craving for learning surfaced. Muniamma *longed* to study. She could read, but there was much she did not know.

'I do have a lot to be thankful for,' she reminded herself as she looked around at the children in the streets. She kept on walking.

Finally, spotting a smooth rock in front of one of the homes, she decided to sit and continue watching the children.

When she noticed an offering of fruit on the ground, she stepped back. She realised she had accidentally ambled into a 'holy' area and that a nearby family must worship this rock as their god, but she did not want to linger or upset anyone by her intrusion.

Just then a young mother came out of the house, her face pale and distressed. 'What are you doing there?' she yelled to Muniamma.

'Nothing,' Muni said. 'Honestly, I was just out for a walk and decided to sit down for a while. I see that this is your holy rock. I will leave.'

The young mother's hands shook nervously, and some of the milk spilled from the brass bowl she held. Muniamma could hear an infant wailing inside the house. She knew the mother was about to add this milk offering to the offerings of fruit already placed in front of the rock.

'Is your baby sick?' she asked gently.

'Yes, oh yes!' the woman sobbed. 'And we don't know what else to do for him.'

Surprisingly, Muniamma was not nervous. 'Please, ma'am, maybe you would let me pray to God for your baby?' Then she felt shocked by her own boldness.

'You're not much more than a child yourself. But yes, please pray. Which god do you pray to?'

'Oh ... I used to p... pray to Kali,' Muniamma began haltingly.

The woman backed away and more milk spilled over the rim of the brass bowl. 'Kali!' the mother exclaimed. 'You're a follower of Kali? I've heard she is a goddess of vengeance and is very powerful. I've always been too afraid to pray to her. If you would be so brave as to pray to Kali for our baby, I would be grateful.'

As they were talking, the husband came to the

84

door with their sick baby in his arms. He looked dishevelled and his eyes were hostile as he stared at the strange young girl in his front yard.

The wife spoke to her husband. 'This girl says she will pray to Kali for us. Maybe Kali will hear her prayers and our son will get better.'

The husband visibly relaxed and swore under his breath. 'For a minute I thought you were one of those I saw with that group of Christians. About an hour ago I saw a truck and van with some white folks come into the barracks. I heard them asking directions to Pastor Moonsami's. You look like the Indian girl in the back of the truck.'

Muniamma moved uncomfortably.

'Christians!' The father spat the word. 'Why don't they just leave us alone?' He swore again.

Muniamma tried to interrupt, but the distraught wife blurted out, 'Please, by all means, pray to Kali for us. We've been praying to our rock god for days, and our son just keeps getting worse. My old mother-in-law has even gone up to Isipingo to the big temple to pray for his healing.' Tears filled her eyes.

The father looked down at his fevered son, then over at their holy rock, and then shook his head at Muni. 'We've never dared pray to Kali before, but we've heard she has great powers. Go ahead and pray to this goddess for us. It might help.'

Muniamma felt desperate. *What should I do?* she

questioned herself. *This whole conversation is completely out of control and they've jumped to the wrong conclusion. They believe I'm a Hindu and a Kali worshipper.* Nervously she bit on her stubby thumbnail.

She hadn't meant this to happen. It wasn't her fault. Should she just walk away and let them believe she was going to her own house to light a prayer lamp and pray to Kali? Would that be right? They were adults and she was just turning fourteen. Wouldn't it be rude if she tried to explain that she was no longer a Kali worshipper but was really a follower of the God of creation? She was a Christian.

While Muniamma stood there thinking, the wife placed the milk offering before her rock god, went to her husband and took the child.

'Hurry,' he demanded of his wife. There was deep concern in his voice. 'Get my son inside the house.'

The wife slowly turned from Muniamma and went inside, anxiously holding their restless baby in her arms.

It was almost too late, and Muniamma felt desperate to make the truth known. Tears came to her eyes. 'Excuse me again. Please!'

The wife turned in the doorway, 'Yes?'

'It is true. I have prayed to Kali in the past. In fact, I had Kali's curse on me. My own father put an awful curse on me when I was born. But now I'm free from Kali's curse; I have a new life.'

'No!' the husband exclaimed. 'That's not possible! No one is ever free from Kali's curse. This goddess is full of revenge, and no one crosses her.'

'I know. Kali almost made me go blind.' Muniamma paused and took a deep breath, trying to talk more slowly. 'One day I heard from my Aunt Sita about a more powerful God than Kali,' Muniamma continued. 'This God healed my eyes and took Kali's curse away.'

'Who is this god? Tell us quickly. Maybe he will heal our son.'

'He is the God of creation. He is the God who made everything and he made you and me. When I heard about him and that he loves all of us, I was surprised, just as you are.'

The husband and wife looked at each other and then back at this strange young girl who spoke so knowledgeably about religious things. Muniamma continued, 'This God doesn't want our sacrifices,' and she quickly glanced down at the coconuts, bananas and milk offerings before their rock god.

'A god that doesn't demand sacrifice and he still heals?' the wife said incredulously. 'A god that loves and created all things? Tell us more!'

'Nonsense!' the husband shouted. 'If there is a god like this we would have heard about him. No Hindu, not even a Hindu priest has told us of such a god. It's too good to be true.'

'This God talked to my grandmother in Tamil.'

'What?' the couple exclaimed.

'He did. She heard him. He said, 'Stop sweeping,

and go to church.' You see, my Ma was sweeping around our Hindu shrine, getting everything ready for her morning prayers, when all of a sudden she heard a voice talking to her in Tamil. She thought someone was playing the fool with her, but no one was. She heard God's voice three times, and each time God said, "Stop sweeping, and go to church."'

'Church? That's where Christians meet.' The wife's voice sounded scared. She clutched her sick baby tightly to her breast.

'Yes, yes it is.' Muniamma quivered.

'So, I was right. I did see you with the Christians!'

'Yes.' Muniamma slowly shook her head, and her voice was barely audible.

'How dare you come here and tell us rubbish at a time like this. How dare you!' the husband shouted.

'I just wanted you to know. I believe it was God's Son, Jesus, who healed my eyes and talked to my grandmother in Tamil. Jesus can help you too.'

The husband put his hands over his ears and shook his head violently. Then he glared directly at Muniamma, and his eyes looked glazed.

Muniamma was frightened and she immediately thought of that one-legged dancer she had seen in the Hindu temple who had slithered her way towards her and Grandmother.

This man had that same horrifying look. 'Don't say that name!' he shouted. 'Get out of here! I will not have you say that name!'

'Jesus?' Muniamma said. She repeated the name out of surprise at the man's reaction, and not because she was trying to defy his demand.

Screaming, the wife turned and ran into the house. At the same moment, the husband picked up a stone and threw it at Muniamma. It hit her square in the shoulder. She cried out in pain. 'Please sir, I didn't mean to make you angry. I want you to know Jesus. He loves you!'

The man became mad with rage and ran towards Muniamma, knocking her on the side of her head. She went flying to the ground. He kicked her twice in the side before she could move away from him.

'Get out of here before he kills you,' the wife yelled from the door. 'Run, girl. Go!'

Muniamma was too frightened to feel much pain, at least for the moment. She turned to run and stumbled. The man kicked her again while she was down, but somehow Muniamma got to her feet, and this time she did not fall. She ran as fast as she could while rocks whizzed past her head.

'How could this have happened?' she sobbed as she kept running. Then she recalled how months earlier, she and Grandmother had thrown oranges at Aunt Sita because of just such a conversation.

'Help!' Muniamma cried as she ran. 'Help!' she screamed. 'Why didn't I just shut up?' she sobbed to herself as she stumbled blindly along. 'Don't I have

She went flying to the ground.

enough problems of my own without making new ones?'

Muniamma did not take time to think these things through. They were just frantic thoughts as she ran for her life.

Chapter Ten

Muniamma did not stop running. She did not even notice that she was no longer being pursued. Her laboured breaths came in great gulps as she painfully dashed down the narrow walkways between the barracks, desperately trying to find her way back. She wasn't even certain which direction she had come, but she kept running anyway.

The old gash above her left eye reopened, and blood slowly oozed out and down her face. Some got into her mouth, and it tasted like copper.

Where the rock had struck it her shoulder hurt, and Muniamma held her arm to support its weight. Her side and back, where the irate father had kicked her, were also beginning to ache. Her long black hair flew everywhere, even into her eyes, but she kept moving.

As she turned a corner, she stumbled right into Ken. The force of the collision knocked Muniamma backwards, and she fell to the ground, gasping for breath.

'Watch it!' Ken yelled. He toppled over, not noticing who it was. 'What's the big idea?'

'It's Muniamma!' Sue yelled in alarm, coming up behind Ken, who was getting quickly to his feet.

Muniamma's eyes were dilated as she frantically looked around. 'Where is he?' she managed to get out between raspy breaths.

'Where's who?' Lou asked. 'Muniamma, you've been hurt!'

'Hurry,' Muni cried. 'He's after me.'

'Who? Your father?' they all asked at once.

Muniamma gulped and shook her head.

The Mortons looked relieved. They wanted nothing to do with Krish or his partner.

'It doesn't look like anyone's after you,' Ken said with a calm voice, though the twins could tell he was far from calm.

They all looked around and saw people beginning to stare at them through their windows. Then they noticed a few brave and very curious onlookers coming out of their homes to join the crowd which was forming, obviously curious about the three white teenagers and their hurt Indian friend. It was also obvious these people had not been chasing Muniamma.

'Whoever was after you is gone,' Sue reassured. 'Now, Muniamma, what's this all about? You've been away from the pastor's house for a long time, and your grandmother sent us to find you. What happened? Why didn't you invite us to come along?'

'This is no place to talk,' Lou said urgently. 'Let's get Muniamma away from all these gawking people. And besides, we need to do something to stop this bleeding.'

'Come,' Ken said, helping Muni to her feet and holding her arm. They walked away from the crowd and went around the side of one of the barracks.

'Over there,' Sue said and pointed to a large tree.

The Mortons helped Muniamma get settled as comfortably as possible in the shade. Lou wrenched off her half-slip and carefully dabbed at the gash above Muni's eye.

'Don't do that!' Sue snapped. 'Hold your hand firmly and apply some pressure. That's better.'

Then Ken interrupted, 'Now, Muniamma, this is very important. I want to help. Tell me who's beaten you up, and I'll go after him. I wish Raneesh were here; he'd come with me!'

'Sparky,' Muniamma moaned. 'If only my dog were here. He would protect me.'

'I'm sure he would,' Ken agreed.

'But he isn't here, and neither is Raneesh,' Sue interrupted. 'But I am—and I want to go with you, Kenny. Muniamma, you are like a sister to me. Nobody is going to beat up my sister.'

'Hold it, you two,' Lou said. 'Nobody is going to go running off and beating up anybody. We need to get Muniamma back to Pastor Moonsami's and let Mum tend to her. Maybe she needs stitches.'

'You take her back,' Ken said irritably. 'Just hang onto her arm and help her walk. The pastor's house is up two barracks and to your left.'

Through this whole exchange, Muniamma had said very little. She was still feeling shaken. Besides,

94

she was genuinely surprised to see how much the Mortons wanted to help, and she felt especially surprised that Ken was being so protective. But she was quite certain that she did not want him to go back and fight that man.

'Muniamma, I want to ask you again,' Ken's voice sounded extremely strained. His straight brown hair, which had been combed neatly to the side, now hung into his eyes. 'Tell me who's done this to you!'

'Don't tell,' Lou pleaded. 'Kenny, you're out of your mind. Stop hammering Muniamma with your questions and help me get her home. You too, Sue.'

'You're always telling us what to do,' Sue said furiously. 'Why don't you stop acting like Mum!'

'Then why don't you stop acting like you always *need* a mother,' Lou retorted.

Ken stood up abruptly. 'Stop it you two. And for what I am about to do, I don't need anybody's help.' He looked meaningfully at Sue. 'I'm going to go and find out for myself who's responsible. I'll find the kid who's done this to Muniamma, and I'll see to him.'

'Please, Kenny,' Muniamma said. The pleading in her voice finally made him turn and stop. 'You don't understand,' she continued through her tears. 'Don't go and try to find him. Please!'

'Why not?' Ken shouted. 'You've had so many bad things happen to you.' There was a catch in his throat. 'It makes me sick. Every time I turn around, something else is happening. You're just like a sister

95

to me too, and I can't stand by and do nothing. This time I can help, and I want to go and find that guy and make him pay for hurting you.'

Muniamma remembered how her brothers had once acted just like Kenny. They had always wanted to protect her, and whenever she got hurt, they were upset.

With tears streaming down her cheeks she said, 'Thank you, Kenny, for caring. I really mean that.'

'Then why don't you let me know what's happened and where this fellow is?'

'Because he isn't a boy, he is ... he is a man.'

The Mortons looked at each other in horror.

'A *man* beat you up?' Ken said as if he couldn't believe his ears.

'Well, he had a reason. You see, I told him about Jesus, and he got mad.'

Sue was the first to respond. 'Do you mean that in the midst of all your troubles, you've been out witnessing?'

'Witnessing?' Muniamma repeated the word slowly. She had heard the term before, but was uncertain of exactly what it meant.

Lou interrupted, 'Why don't you just tell us what happened? Begin at the beginning when you left Pastor Moonsami's.'

Muniamma related her story. Ken and the twins listened intently to every word. When she began to speak about the distraught parents and how they thought she still worshipped Kali, Sue admitted, 'I think I would have let them draw their own conclusions. I don't believe I would have had the nerve to

96

tell them the truth.'

'Wow!' Lou exclaimed. 'What did the father do after you told him you pray to Jesus, not Kali?'

Muni didn't answer right away.

'Tell us,' Ken encouraged. 'Is that when the father hit you?'

She shook her head.

Ken stood up. 'That makes me so mad! Why doesn't he pick on someone his own size? He must be a big bully.'

'He was upset about his baby,' Lou defended. 'Calm down, Kenny.'

'Don't tell me to calm down.'

Once again Muniamma began crying. Sue glared at her brother and sister for upsetting Muni. 'Have some consideration,' she said. Protectively she put her arm around Muni's thin shoulders and pulled her close. Muni winced. The sleeve of her good dress was dirty and torn, and Muniamma rubbed the spot to try and ease the pain.

Lou had previously tied her slip around Muniamma's head, and a small spot of blood had soaked through onto the white nylon. But it looked as if the bleeding had stopped.

Lou touched Muni's hand. 'You did the right thing, even though it was hard. You are such a good example to me. You were honest to those parents. I hope their baby will be all right. We should pray for him.'

Sue also looked at Muni with admiration, 'You were certainly brave, Muniamma. That baby's father still makes me mad though! His being upset is no excuse for hitting you.'

Muniamma hung her head. She didn't feel one bit brave. The fact of her running away from the baptismal service should have been proof enough. *How can they think I'm brave and a good Christian when I'm always scared?* she wondered. *I'm not only scared of that man back there, but I'm terrified of my own father and his partner.* She wanted to voice these thoughts, but couldn't.

Ken marched back and forth in front of the three girls. The more he marched, the angrier he became. 'I wasn't allowed to help last week. Raneesh and I had it all planned how we were going to rescue you. But nothing worked out. Well, this time I'm going to help. That man can't get away with hitting you. After Dad finds out, we'll both go back there and find him and tell him just what we think.'

'We'll see,' Lou said thoughtfully. 'Meanwhile, let's get Muniamma back so Mum can take care of her.'

Together, the four teenagers walked the rest of the way to Pastor Moonsami's home, Muniamma limping slightly because of all the bruises. Each was deep in thought, but no one trusted himself enough to put his thoughts into words.

How would Muni's grandmother respond? What would Aunt Sita and Uncle say? Would Pastor Moonsami and his wife know these people who had a sick baby? Would all the Christians join together and fight this mean man who would dare to strike a helpless girl?

All these questions plagued the young people as they turned the corner and went silently to Pastor Moonsami's home.

Chapter Eleven

Meanwhile, Kathie and Vino, the teenage daughter of one of the new Christian families, were helping some of the women in the outside kitchen with the dishes. Large enamel basins had been placed on an old wooden table and each was filled with cold water. Surrounding the basins were piles of dirty, greasy dishes.

Aunt Sita had her hands in one of the tubs and was scrubbing the plates with a square piece of orange mesh material. Every once in a while she'd stop and rub a bar of green soap with the mesh until it lathered and then go back to scrubbing the plates. Several times Sita nonchalantly shoved aside the coagulated grease which was collecting on top of the water and then proceeded with her scouring.

Kathie stared in fascination. Never had doing the dishes been so interesting.

When Aunt Sita felt the plate was clean, she'd hand it to Pastor Moonsami's wife, Indra, who'd rinse it in the second basin of cold water and hand it to either Kathie or Vino to dry.

The dishes were just about finished when Kathie

looked up and saw Ken, the twins and Muniamma coming around the distant corner of the long barracks.

'Hey, everyone...they're back!' Kathie yelled so everyone could hear. She looked at Vino and whispered, 'That's just like my brother and little sisters. They always show up after the work is done.'

'I know what you mean, my brothers never have to do as much work as I do. See—they've already run home to play. Life is so easy for them.'

Kathie sighed, thinking of what her mother would say sometimes. She murmured to Vino, 'A woman's work is never done.'

'We are women, are we?' her friend responded, and they both giggled.

Then Kathie took a closer look down the walkway. 'Something's wrong!' she yelled. Dropping the tea towel, she began running towards the group. 'What's happened? You all look awful. Muniamma, you're hurt!'

'Get Mum,' Ken said urgently.

Just then Mary Morton came to the door of the pastor's home. She had spent a quiet afternoon with the two new Christian families and had just heard again Poonamah's story about how God miraculously talked to her in Tamil. Everyone had been encouraged. An evening church service of songs and praise had been planned, and all the Christians in the barracks had been invited to join them. Mary had been anxious that her children should return and wash before the evening service.

'Hurry!' Kathie exclaimed as she met her mother

in the doorway. 'Muniamma's been hurt.'

'Oh my goodness!' Mrs Morton exclaimed. Immediately, she took charge. 'Get her inside and into bed,' she said to the twins. 'Kathie, boil water and find some clean towels.'

As soon as they entered the house, Poonamah wailed, 'What's happened to my baby?'

For a moment, Muniamma wondered what Ma meant, then realised she must look an awful sight to get such a reaction.

Carefully, Grandmother and the twins helped Muni to the bed. Aunt Sita put her arm around Poonamah, and they hovered close to the bedside looking at the pitiful figure. Muniamma's dress was torn and dirty. She was clutching her shoulder, and the blood seeping through the half-slip did not look reassuring.

Sue said excitedly, with tears in her eyes, 'Oh, Mummy, is Muniamma going to be all right?'

'Yes, sweetie. She'll be fine.' Mary gently removed the knotted slip and looked closely at Muni's forehead. 'Oh, gracious, this doesn't look good...but at least the bleeding has stopped. I'll put on a butterfly bandage after we've cleaned it. There's nowhere around here to get stitches.'

Muniamma nodded.

Then Mrs Morton looked more intently at Muniamma. 'I'm afraid this reopened gash is going to leave a scar. I don't think it will be too noticeable, but....'

What did Aunt Sita say about scars? Muniamma wondered as the missionary began cleaning her wound.

Something about scars of the heart? Anyway, she continued thinking, *I don't mind a scar on my forehead if it means Raj won't want to marry me.*

Suddenly Mrs Morton interrupted her thoughts, 'There, that's better. Now let me take a look at your shoulder.'

Everyone had been holding back a flood of questions, but as soon as Grandmother saw Muni's shoulder with the beginnings of a large bruise, she demanded in a quivering voice, 'What happened?'

By this time the room was full. Aunt Sita and Uncle, Pastor Moonsami and his wife and all the Mortons were crowded around the bed. 'Did you fall?' Grandmother asked anxiously.

'A man tried to kill her!' It was Ken who spoke, and for a moment there was a shocked silence. Then the silence in the room exploded with everyone talking at the same time.

'Quiet!' Poonamah shouted. 'I want to know what's happened to my granddaughter. I want her to tell us in her own words exactly what went on this afternoon. I want to know if my son, Krish, had anything to do with this.'

Muniamma quickly covered her shoulder and pulled the thick quilt up under her chin. Staring down at the intricate pattern of the hand-made quilt, she answered self-consciously, 'No, Ma, this time Father had nothing to do with what happened.'

'Was it that awful partner of his that did this to you? You know, that man Raj?'

'No, Ma.'

The last thing Muniamma wanted to do was to

retell her story about the events of the afternoon. But there was no way around it; everyone stood waiting.

Hesitantly, Muniamma began, and once again everyone listened intently.

Finally, Pastor Moonsami spoke, 'I know who you are talking about. That man and his old mother have given my wife and me a lot of trouble, especially that old Mrs Reddy. She hates Christians. In fact, I heard a couple of days ago that she went up to Isipingo to say prayers at the big temple for the healing of her grandson. Maybe you have seen her this past week? She is usually very argumentative around Christians and makes her presence known. Believe me, Mrs Reddy speaks against us every chance she gets.'

Once again a stupefying silence spread across the room. Each person knew exactly whom he meant.

'We've met her,' Aunt Sita said gravely.

Muniamma covered her face with trembling hands and began crying.

'Now...now,' Mary Morton said gently, and took Muniamma's hands away from the freshly applied bandage. 'You need to be careful. You certainly wouldn't want that to reopen and start bleeding again.'

Sue and Lou sat on the edge of the bed, and they both reached out to touch Muni.

Pastor Moonsami continued, 'I honestly think that old Mrs Reddy has a bad spirit. Possibly the father of that sick baby is troubled by spirits too.'

Muniamma broke into a cold sweat.

Aunt Sita stepped forward. 'Think, Muniamma, did you notice anything strange about the baby's father?'

Ken interrupted, 'You bet she noticed something strange—he hit her!'

The Mortons looked horrified.

'Calm down son,' Mary admonished. 'Nothing will be solved by your bad temper.'

Mr Morton frowned at his son, then looked over at Muniamma. 'Tell us if you noticed anything odd.'

Muni was weary of talking and questions. She desperately wished everyone would go away and just let her cry. Every day her life seemed to become more complicated. She realised, however, that the adults would not stop asking questions until they knew everything there was to know about the situation. She noticed Grandmother's worried expression as she leaned against the foot of the bed. Ma nodded encouragement.

'Well,' Muni began hesitantly, 'this may not mean anything, but it *was* strange.'

Everyone waited. Even Ken stopped pacing and looked at Muni. Ma nodded again for Muni to continue.

'When I mentioned the name of Jesus, the father put his hands over his ears and demanded I not say that name. I didn't understand, and I repeated Jesus' name. That's when he got mad, knocked me down and started throwing rocks.'

'Humph,' Pastor Moonsami said, his dark face round and thoughtful. 'Not wanting to hear the name Jesus is a definite sign of a bad spirit.'

'That's no excuse!' Ken's voice was unnaturally loud, almost a shout. 'He's a grown man and he hit a girl. He's a big bully! We should go back there and make him regret his actions.'

'Yeah,' Sue agreed. She jumped up and stood beside Ken.

'Lower your voices, you two,' their father demanded. 'There's no need for you to yell. We're all sympathetic to your feelings, but nothing is ever solved through anger; it only makes the matter worse.'

'Daddy's right,' Mary said to her children.

'But I do agree with Ken in one way,' Mr Morton admitted. 'I believe we should go and find that man.'

Every person in the room looked surprised.

'Why?' Uncle asked. He was standing close to Aunt Sita at the door.

'Isn't it obvious? We need to go and cast out those bad spirits. And when we get back to Isipingo we need to confront Mrs Reddy. I think we should also deal more forcefully with Krish and his partner, Raj. This whole situation is getting out of control.'

'Not so fast,' Pastor Moonsami said to the missionary and smiled understandingly. 'I believe we need to spend time in prayer before we do anything.'

'By all means!' Missionary Morton agreed heartily. 'We need to pray, and then we need to go over and confront this problem properly.'

'Well, let's see how God directs,' the Indian pastor said. 'Who knows, God may bring these troubled people right to our very door.'

Muniamma shivered and pulled the quilt to her

mouth. She bit down on the material.

Mary Morton smoothed Muni's dishevelled hair and said, 'I think someone should go immediately to find out how that sick baby is doing.'

The rest of the Mortons agreed.

Once again Pastor Moonsami responded. 'Your concern is commendable, but first we need prayer protection before we go headlong into the frontline of the battle.'

Soon, each would realise Pastor Moonsami's wisdom.

Chapter Twelve

Back on the other side of the barracks, the unhappy young Mrs Reddy faced her husband. She held her baby close to her breast and said nervously, 'You shouldn't have done that. You shouldn't have hit that girl.'

'She had no business coming here!'

The young wife knew better than to antagonise her husband. She was painfully acquainted with his violent fits of anger. It was terrifying how both he and his old mother became unreasonably angry ... sometimes with very little cause.

'Christians!' Mr Reddy said, and spat on the floor. 'They never mean any harm, but that's all they cause. My mother is right: we were better off before any of us heard about this Christian rubbish. We were meant to be Hindus. Whoever heard of Indians becoming Christians? That's the white man's religion.'

'I know,' his wife agreed and swallowed nervously. She shifted the weight of her son in her arms. His thin arms and legs thrashed about. 'B... but that young girl said that the Christian God talked to her old Ma in Tamil. I don't understand.'

'What is there to understand? It's a big lie!'

'I...I wonder,' she continued hesitantly. 'She said this God is more powerful than Kali and that he created everything and he...er...actually talked to her Ma in Tamil! The old woman was r...ready to say her morning prayers. She s...sounds like she was a devout Hindu. Why would this God tell her to stop sweeping and go to church?'

'Don't be stupid!' By now her husband was shouting loudly. 'That didn't happen. It's all in her imagination. Stories like these are told to mislead simple people. I don't believe a word that girl said. Now forget it and get me something to eat.'

The mother knew better than to say any more so she carried her son into the bedroom and laid him on the old mattress which had been pushed back in the corner. He was hot to the touch, but not sweaty. 'I'm scared,' she admitted out loud. 'You've just got to get better.' Tears spilled over and dropped onto the feverish skin of her precious son.

Just then the father leaned against the door of the bedroom, 'I'll stay with him while you make the curry. He shouldn't be left alone.'

His wife nodded and silently left the room. She hated to leave and cook at a time like this, but she also knew her husband was right; they needed to eat and keep up their strength.

With great reluctance, she went across the walkway to her open kitchen and lit the kerosene burner. Mechanically, she pounded garlic and ginger to add to the hot oil which was in the pot. Then she chopped onions and tomatoes and added them. Finally, she put in several tablespoons of her curry spices and let the steaming mixture cook while she cut the cabbage. Even her favourite meal, curried cabbage, didn't seem good today.

While the meal simmered, the spicy smell filled the kitchen. Rice boiled in another big pot on another burner. 'Maybe if I go and say some more prayers to my god, my baby will get better,' she thought. Tears came again to her eyes and she wiped them with a handkerchief she always kept stuffed down the front of her sari blouse.

She went to her lounge and picked up a brass bell which was kept on a shelf in the corner of the room. She hurried outside to the front yard and knelt before her rock god.

The rock looked ordinary. It was about the size of a small oval roasting pan but it was flat and smooth. It had been placed in their front yard under the big tree by her mother-in-law, who had brought it from India and claimed it was holy.

They had said their prayers before that rock for several years now, and it had been good to them. Every week the young wife had bathed the rock and put offerings before it.

Since praying to the rock god, her husband had had a steady job at the sugar mill and had even received several promotions. He would have been working again today, but the mill was closed for repairs.

Their prayers for a son had also been answered by this god. *Yes, this rock god has been good to us. So what is the matter?* the young mother questioned in her heart.

In desperation, she knelt. She held the little brass bell in her hands and shook it. If the spirit behind the rock god was asleep or away, she wanted to gain his attention. She shook the bell again and waited, hoping her god would come and hear her prayers. Then the troubled mother pulled the end of her sari over her head and began praying in Tamil. With tears streaming down her face, over and over she repeated her plea for the life of their son.

Suddenly a disturbing thought interrupted her prayers. It was something that Muniamma had said about the God of creation loving them. *Could this be true?* she questioned and opened her eyes, staring at the rock god. *Could this god love? It does not have eyes, so it cannot see. It doesn't even have ears to hear. Was there truly a God like the young girl talked about that made everything and loves people? A God that would not demand offerings and sacrifices? But what did this have to do with Christians and someone they called Jesus?*

Nothing made sense. Nevertheless, the young mother had a longing in her heart to know such a God.

'What would my mother-in-law do if she knew I was even thinking this way?' she mumbled to herself. She felt confused about her husband's mother. One minute she could be sweet and kind, and the next minute bitter and hateful.

'But today,' the distraught mother spoke out loud to reassure herself, 'my mother-in-law is being kind.

She began praying in Tamil.

She is in Isipingo right now saying prayers in the temple. If that doesn't help our son to get better, nothing will!'

Frantically, young Mrs Reddy continued reciting prayers to the rock god. She didn't know how long she stayed. This was often the case. Once she began saying prayers, she went into some sort of state where she completely lost touch with reality. This time, however, she was shaken out of her trance-like state by her husband.

'Quick! Come!'

For a brief moment, his wife froze. Instinctively she knew their baby was worse. Her inaction only lasted a moment, then adrenalin shot through her veins and she got up and dashed into the house. Their baby lay silent in the corner, and at first she thought he was dead.

'My baby!' she screamed. 'He's dead!'

'No...he's not dead. See...he's still breathing, but something awful is happening.'

The mother saw. Her baby was no longer restless, but was lying listlessly. His eyes were rolled back and all they could see was the whites against the dark skin of his delicate face.

Suddenly the baby's head began to jerk, and then his arms and legs began shaking violently. Finally his whole body began to twitch. It was a dreadful sight, and the parents stared in horror.

The mother scooped up her precious son and tried to make him stop. 'Oh, stop, stop!' she pleaded. 'Oh, make him stop,' she cried to her husband.

But the baby was powerless, as was his father. 'I don't know what to do,' he cried desperately. 'I've never seen anything like this.'

The mother began wailing. The sound was totally devastating and there was a lostness to the tone which sent chills down her husband's back. The mother clutched her twisting and jerking infant to her bosom and capered around the room like a wild woman.

Mr Reddy knew he must act quickly or he would lose both his son and his wife. If his old mother were here, she would know what to do. She always knew what prayers to say or what offerings to give. But she was gone. *Maybe I should go to our temple,* he thought. But then he remembered that the mill was closed and most people were away; even the priest was gone for the weekend.

'What should we do?' he asked aloud. His wife did not hear him. Completely frantic, she went on wailing at a high pitch.

It started gradually. Mr Reddy had experienced these sensations before and they had never ceased to shock and fill him with horror. It was as if something alien was taking over his body—his whole being. It felt as if a presence from deep inside, some grossly evil thing, stirred. It moved around, yearning to destroy.

Mr Reddy never knew exactly when he lost control of himself or when this presence took over. All he knew was that something evil would enter and possess his body, and he hated it.

Suddenly his eyes became vacant-looking and his

114

body stiffened. A guttural voice, unlike his own, interrupted his wife's screaming, 'Christians! It's their fault! I'll make that Christian girl pay. I'll make them all pay!'

He grabbed a blanket, dashed to his frightened wife, and took the baby out of her arms. Thus far, the dreadful twisting and jerking of their son had lasted less than a minute, but to the parents it had seemed like hours.

'Where are you going?' the mother screeched, tearing out some of her hair. 'Give me back my baby!' Then she saw her husband's face, grotesquely contorted, and she shivered, momentarily falling back against the wall.

Mr Reddy did not stop to answer. He started for the kitchen and picked up a huge butcher's knife. In his rage, he knocked the simmering pot off the burner, and curried cabbage spilled everywhere.

'What are you doing?' she shrieked in total panic. 'Where are you going with my baby and that knife?'

Again, he did not answer but began running down the narrow pathway between the barracks, his wife stumbling after him, screaming all the way. In the midst of everything, the baby's body went limp and lay in his father's arms as if dead. Fury filled the father even more, and he ran faster.

People came out of their houses and stared. Others quickly darted back behind their doors, not wanting to get involved.

Down the pathway they ran. Mr Reddy was

beyond rational thinking. 'They are to blame for everything!' he bellowed.

He ran as if his life depended upon it...and it did, and so did the life of his son.

Chapter Thirteen

For a moment, Muniamma closed her eyes and nestled deeper into the soft folds of Pastor and Mrs Moonsami's bed. The murmur of the surrounding prayers began to calm her racing heart. As the prayers continued, Muniamma's breathing slowed and her taut muscles began to relax. The throbbing in her head and shoulders eased.

Sue and Lou had been closely watching their friend, and at this first encouraging sign Sue looked over at her sister and raised her eyebrows. Lou smiled in return and then nodded towards Ken.

They both glanced over to where their brother was standing. Almost everyone else in the crowded bedroom was kneeling in fervent prayer, but Ken stood back almost behind the bedroom door. He was restless; the twins could hear him moving his weight from one foot to the other. Lou pursed her lips and shook her head.

Ken knew his sisters had been watching. It was difficult to explain, but he sensed it without looking. He absolutely hated the helpless, frustrating feeling that settled over him. *I always felt in control when I was back in England,* he thought. *Why has everything turned so upside down since we've come here to South Africa? Why can't life just be easy for a change?'*

He kicked his foot against the wall and his soled shoe hit harder than he expected. Immediately, Ken knew the sound had made several more people look his way. 'Good going,' he mumbled irritably. *If I could just get out of here,* he thought. *I could settle the score with that father. Having a sick baby is no excuse for being a bully!*

Pastor Moonsami spoke, 'Listen, everyone.' The prayers stopped and even Ken looked over to where the Indian pastor stood. The buttons on his waistcoat had come undone and his round potbelly stuck out. 'I believe we are not fighting against flesh and blood. Our real enemy is not Mr Reddy or any other human. I believe very strongly that this battle is against principalities and powers and rulers of the darkness.'

Sure, Ken thought, even as chills ran down his back. *I suppose Muniamma's forehead was not really bleeding.* He wanted to say this, but didn't dare.

Uncle and Aunt Sita agreed with Pastor Moonsami, and so did Ken's parents.

'We have no choice,' the Indian pastor continued. 'We have not sought out this battle. The enemy presses us to it. God's will is that we put on the armour he has provided and fight a good fight.'

Muniamma's panic returned. She wanted to run,

not fight. She glanced at Grandmother, who had been kneeling by the side of the bed. Ma looked perplexed about this talk of armour and Muni noticed the beads of perspiration lining the coarse hairs on Ma's upper lip. Nevertheless, Poonamah stared bravely into her granddaughter's terrified eyes. 'Are you ready for yet another battle?' they seemed to say.

Sue and Lou reached out and grasped Muniamma's hands. She did not look their way, but kept staring at her grandmother, trying to gain courage.

Pastor Moonsami noticed the pathetic look and he stepped forward and prayed with outstretched arms, 'In the name of Jesus Christ, I ask that you cover this house with your protection. Please do not allow even one of your children to get harmed in the battle ahead. Surround this home with your angels and do not permit evil to enter.'

The twins squeezed harder, and even Ken's shuffling stopped.

Then Uncle's voice rang out, 'I agree with my Christian brother. In the name of Jesus Christ and under the authority of the blood of Jesus, I command any evil spirits who may be present to leave us alone. I do not command this in my own authority, but in the authority of Jesus' holy name.'

Just then a piercing scream broke the ensuing silence. It came from outside. 'Don't!' a woman screeched. 'Watch out, you Christians! He's got a knife!'

'Shut up!' the man yelled and thrust his sick baby into the woman's arms. 'I'm going to kill them,' he vowed. 'I'm going to kill that girl and then I'm going to slash every one of those Christians!'

'No!' Mrs Reddy cried, desperately hugging her baby. 'Stop! You don't know what you're doing! You've gone completely mad!'

The husband shoved his frightened wife aside and ran for the front door of Pastor Moonsami's home.

At first, the Christians were stunned. No one moved. Everyone stayed deathly still, like stone statues. It wasn't until the first sound of something hitting the door that everyone jumped.

Muniamma leapt up, throwing aside the covers, and clawed her way under the bed. Sue and Lou followed. All three lay huddled together, barely breathing.

Ma and Aunt Sita crouched behind an over-stuffed chair.

Ken stayed behind the bedroom door and his face looked drained of colour as he tried to push his body into the wall.

The noise everyone heard was Mr Reddy pulling off the wooden cross that Pastor Moonsami and Indra had hung on their front door. He kept banging the cross against the house until it splintered and broke. An unholy hate filled his whole being and vile words spewed from his mouth. It did not sound as if the words came from Mr Reddy at all, but from something evil living down inside, straining to get out.

Muniamma could hear all the Christians praying, even the twins. They were pleading, 'In the name of Jesus, hold that door closed! Don't let him come in! Hold that door!'

Nearly everyone was sobbing, but no one went over to make sure the door was even shut. Most of the men were standing together in the middle of the room, praying. Muniamma wanted someone to pile furniture in front of the door and also at the windows, but the Christians seemed immobile.

Muni knew she must have bumped her forehead yet again because blood began oozing out from around the bandage, and a huge drop trickled down and plopped onto the floor, right in front of her eyes. She stared at her own blood, and her entire body went numb with fear.

Frantically she peeped out from under the bed. To her horror she could see that the front door was actually open about the width of a couple of fingers. Nothing was keeping her enemy away. She knew without a doubt that it would take no effort at all for the baby's father to push open the door and come in.

Yet no one moved. Everyone kept praying. The plea, 'Jesus, hold that door!' echoed around the room.

Suddenly Mr Reddy laughed wickedly. The wooden cross lay in splinters at his feet. Then he turned his full attention towards the pastor's home. 'I'm coming,' he sneered, and laughed again. Finally, he began to push on the door. He pushed, kicked and clawed. 'What's going on?' a voice growled from deep within his throat. Grasping the edge of the door, he began shoving with all his strength. Muniamma could see his fingers and even the tip of the long butcher's knife protruding into the room. Absolutely nothing visible was stopping him from entering.

'Keep holding it, Jesus,' Grandmother cried.

Aunt Sita added, 'For God has not given us the spirit of fear, but of power, and of love, and of a sound mind.'

'Yes, Jesus,' everyone agreed in reverence.

The battle raged. Mr Reddy kept pushing at the open door and even tried prising it farther open with his foot. But some unseen power held it firm. The door did not budge.

'Wow!' Ken exclaimed after several minutes. There was awe in his hushed tone. 'We are actually seeing a miracle!'

'Jesus is holding it, isn't he?' Sue whispered.

Ken gulped and kept staring.

The tug-of-war went on and on. The sick baby's distraught mother kept crying, 'Stop! Someone come and help my baby!' But the father irrationally continued hurling abuse and pushing with all his wild strength.

Uncle's voice rang out, 'Fear is the opposite of faith. This man is not our enemy. Satan is, but we must not fear him. Remember, everyone, the victory of Christ over Satan is total and complete.'

Lou breathlessly said something, but Muniamma

did not hear. The thought of how Jesus shed his blood on the cross came booming into her mind. She looked in wonder from the miracle at the door back down to the drop of blood, drying on the linoleum floor in front of her. Somehow it seemed symbolic: Jesus had shed his blood to save all mankind from eternal death, and now it looked as if Jesus was going to save them from the hand of Mr Reddy. Then she thought of how Jesus was left with many scars; on his back, hands, feet, side and all across his forehead. She touched her own forehead and felt the blood oozing out from around the freshly applied bandage. 'Scars, oh Jesus, you had so many! Thank you, thank you, Jesus!'

Others heard and, at first, they were startled.

'That's right, child,' Grandmother said, her voice quivering with deep emotion. 'We all should thank Jesus for what he has done and for what he is doing right now!'

Just as the Christians began to give praise, there was a sudden silence outside the door. Then Mrs Reddy's scream pierced the air, 'Help! Something's happened to my husband!'

Pastor Moonsami, Uncle and Mr Morton ran to the door and as they got there it swung inwards, Mr Reddy's tall, slender body sprawling across the threshold. The knife dropped from his open hand.

'He's passed out,' Pastor Moonsami shouted. 'Hurry and see to that baby,' he added to the ladies.

Mary Morton and the others carefully stepped over Mr Reddy's still form and rushed to the mother's side. She willingly handed her son over to the missionary, pleading desperately, 'Is it too late?'

Chapter Fourteen

Muniamma and the Morton twins slid out from under the bed. The late afternoon sun filtered in through the threadbare curtains and reflected off the sharp point of the stainless steel blade. It lay within reach of Mr Reddy's unconscious form. Muniamma stumbled backwards against the bed. Then, flopping down, she buried her face in her trembling hands and began to sob.

Uncle stepped over and gently laid his hand on her heaving shoulders. 'I know it's been awful for you, but now is not the time to give in to your fears. The worst of the battle is still ahead.'

'That's right,' Pastor Moonsami added. 'If Satan can create fear in you, you are a much easier prey for him to destroy.'

Ken kicked at the door. 'She's only crying. Most girls would go hysterical at a time like this. Good grief, give her a break!'

'Ken!' Mr Morton admonished sternly. 'We've all been under a lot of tension here. Don't add to it. You take your sisters and Muniamma and go outside.'

Pastor Moonsami shook his head. 'I agree. You children should be out of the room when we deal with the evil spirits which possess Mr Reddy.'

Muniamma stared down at her pursuer. He was beginning to stir, and Muni wanted to get away as fast as she could.

Pastor Moonsami looked squarely at Ken, at the wide-eyed twins and Muniamma, and then around at the men in the room. 'The snarling, wicked powers of darkness will do all they can to intimidate and frighten every one of us in the encounter ahead.'

Muniamma shivered and desperately tried to hold back another sob.

'As believers,' he continued, 'we are to be bold in taking the armour and putting it on. Every time we face the enemy and battle with him we should be sure our armour is in place.'

Ken felt irritated at all this talk about armour, which he did not understand. The twins didn't understand the pastor's comments, either, and they frowned.

Mr Morton put his arm around his son and looked at his twin daughters and then at Muniamma. 'You are not ready for all this. I want you four to stay outside the house until we've dealt with these evil spirits. Help the women with the baby, or better yet, pray.'

'That's right,' Uncle added. 'Pray. And even if you hear strange noises and commotion from in here, don't come in. This is no place for curiosity seekers. Just keep praying.'

'Are you going to be all right, Daddy?' Lou asked, swallowing hard to keep from crying. She had the shivers, and so did Sue.

'Yeah, Dad,' Ken interjected. 'None of us is used to this kind of stuff.'

Mr Morton tried to nod reassuringly, but his children were not fooled; he too was nervous.

Suddenly, from the floor, Mr Reddy moaned. Everyone jumped.

'Hurry, children,' Pastor Moonsami commanded. 'Outside!'

As the young people stepped cautiously around Mr Reddy's body, they heard the Indian pastor saying, 'This man has to want to be delivered before we can do anything. If he desires to keep these evil spirits, then....'

Meanwhile, Mary Morton had been tending to the sick baby. When the young people were outside they looked towards the kitchen. The infant was stripped naked and held lovingly in a basin of tepid water. The women had all crowded around and were speaking in hushed tones. Kathie and her new friend, Vino, were standing back away from the circle. Their heads were together and their lips were moving silently.

'What the baby had was a convulsion,' Mary explained patiently to the weeping mother. 'That sometimes happens with a high fever.'

As the missionary lady continued to explain about convulsions, Aunt Sita and Indra attempted to comfort Mrs Reddy by patting her shoulders. 'Please stop crying,' Sita said. 'This white lady is a trained

127

nurse, and she knows what she's doing.'

'That's right,' Grandmother added. 'She helped my granddaughter, Muniamma, when she had the measles, a high fever, swollen eyes and all sorts of problems.'

Mary smiled at Aunt Sita, Poonamah and the Indian pastor's wife. The ordeal they had just endured had bonded them. 'You are good friends. Thank you.' Then she looked down at the sick baby in the basin. 'Hey...I believe his temperature is beginning to go down. Look here, the little chap is opening his eyes.'

All the ladies leaned over, and a view of the baby was suddenly hidden from the teenagers.

'Kathie, please hurry up and get the medicine in my handbag,' her mother said. 'I brought some baby medicine along today because Shelley wasn't feeling well. It's in a small yellow bottle, right down on the side.'

Kathie rushed over to her mother's handbag, and Shelley whined and pulled on her skirt. Kathie picked up her little sister and handed her into Vino's outstretched arms.

'Now take out one of those tablets and break it up in a clean bowl. We will only need about one quarter of that pill.'

Everyone waited until Kathie had done as she was instructed. 'Now, dissolve it in some of that water,' Mary nodded her head towards the kettle on the burner.

Mrs Reddy stammered, 'Is my baby r...really going to live?'

'Yes, dear,' Mary reassured. 'We are going to drop some of this medicine carefully into his mouth. Here, help me. Let's lean him back, slightly. That's it. Now help me give him a small amount of this medicine.'

When the infant gulped and screwed up his face, everyone breathed a sigh of relief. Finally, he began to whimper, and Mrs Reddy nervously laughed, 'Oh, that sounds so good!'

Lou nudged Ken. 'Do you think we should start praying?'

Ken shrugged his shoulders.

'Please, Kenny,' Sue begged.

Ken walked over to the side of the house and leaned against the rough finish of the window frame. The twins and Muniamma followed.

'Should we pray out loud?' Sue asked.

Ken self-consciously looked down at his scuffed shoes and thought, *Why do I feel so embarrassed? What's wrong with me? Why do I have such a hard time praying in front of others?*

Unexpectedly, Muniamma whispered, 'Jesus... Jesus.' Her head was bowed, eyes closed, with tears streaming down her soft brown cheeks and dripping off her dimpled chin. The Mortons looked at each other. They could not tell if Muniamma was just saying Jesus' name or praying. They felt uncomfortable in the silence that followed.

Finally, Lou prayed, 'We all saw it, God. We all know you held that door closed and you wouldn't let Mr Reddy come in and hurt us.'

'Yes,' Sue mumbled.

Ken nodded his head.

'Help us to trust you right now,' Lou added. 'And ...and please help the sick baby.'

'And help Daddy,' Sue said breathlessly. 'And the rest of the men who are talking with that...that awful Mr Reddy.'

Then Muniamma prayed. 'I think when I was under the jacaranda tree—you *were* there.'

The Mortons looked at each other.

'Even if I didn't believe you were caring for me—you were.'

Ken coughed, and the twins fidgeted.

'And then this afternoon when Mr Reddy knocked me down and kicked me—you were there too, even if I didn't think so at the time.'

The three Mortons bowed their heads.

Muniamma continued, 'But just a few minutes ago, inside this house, you held the door closed and wouldn't let Mr Reddy in to hurt me or any of us. Forgive me for doubting you when I can't see you at work.'

The Mortons hung their heads.

During the resulting silence, they heard Pastor Moonsami's voice through the open window. 'The Lord Jesus Christ is present. Dear Saviour, the wicked spirit that controls this man is insulting you and he is insulting us, your servants. He refuses to leave at our command. I ask you now in your presence to put your holy hand against this demon and send him to the place you have prepared for him. I pray this under the authority of your precious blood.'

Sue and Lou leaned closer to their brother. 'It's weird, isn't it?' Ken whispered. 'Keep praying!'

They could hear commotion inside the house and then a low, guttural sound.

Muniamma felt faint. The twins held on to her, and they all prayed harder.

Uncle's quiet and assured voice interrupted their pleas, 'In the name of Jesus Christ, I bind all you evil spirits together. You may not hurt Mr Reddy when you leave his body. I command you to go now. Go to the pit prepared for you in the name of the Lord Jesus Christ.'

At that instant, Mr Reddy let out a horrid scream.

To the children's surprise, the men in the house began to sing. The words drifted out of the house and even the women across in the kitchen stopped and listened. 'There is power, power, wonder working power, in the blood...of the lamb....'

The teenagers stood huddled, holding hands. Tears stung Ken's eyes, and slowly one tear escaped and began to roll down his face. He did not even try to wipe it away.

'It's weird and wonderful!' Sue said softly.

Then another song rang out, 'What can wash away my sin? Nothing but the blood of Jesus. What can make me whole again? Nothing but the blood of Jesus....'

Muniamma let go of her friends' hands and gently touched the bandage on her forehead. The blood had dried, and she lightly let her fingers trace the outline of the butterfly bandage.

131

The men were coming out of the house, and everyone was shocked by Mr Reddy's changed appearance. His eyes were no longer wild, and his distorted expression had been changed into a gentle look.

Muniamma heard Mr Reddy admit, 'I've always hated it. Ever since I was a boy I have been troubled by bad spirits. You have no idea what it has been like. It's been dreadful! I desperately longed to be rid of them many times, but I had finally given up hope.'

Pastor Moonsami smiled and shook his head, 'You'd be surprised how many of us have been troubled by the same thing. Some day we will share our stories with you and your wife. Only with Jesus Christ is there hope.'

Aunt Sita admitted, 'I had lots of problems with demons, too. Oh, don't look so surprised,' she said when Mrs Reddy's mouth dropped open. 'It's true, I was controlled by evil spirits for many years. Then the day they were commanded to leave, I prayed to the God of creation and asked him to forgive me and come fill me with his Holy Spirit.'

'I want that!' Mr Reddy said. There was genuine excitement in his voice. He hurried over and stood next to his wife. Then, reaching out to the basin, he touched his crying son. 'He looks so much better!' Then to everyone's surprise, he plucked the fussing baby out of the water and held the naked boy high in the air. 'Thank you...thank you!' he cried.

A hush fell over the crowd. After a few seconds, his wife handed him the blanket and everyone watched as they dried their son and wrapped him warmly.

Eventually, the adults gathered together and decided to go into the house to pray. As they entered, Mr Reddy's foot hit the butcher knife, and it skidded across the worn linoleum. 'I certainly won't be needing this,' he said and picked it up. He walked over to Muniamma and handed her the knife.

Muniamma stared from the knife to the man. Everyone waited. It was dusk and grey shadows hung over the scene. Indra quietly lit a kerosene lantern and its light flickered and danced off the stainless steel blade. Still everyone waited. With a quivering hand, Muniamma reached out and grasped hold of the wooden handle. They each held the knife for long moments; Mr Reddy the blade, and Muniamma the handle.

'Victory!' Pastor Moonsami shouted.

Cheers rose towards heaven.

'Allow me to give one word of warning while we are all together,' continued the Indian pastor, his voice rising to a crescendo. 'May we never boast except in the cross of our Lord Jesus Christ. To God be all the glory!'

At that, the twins, Muniamma and even Ken whispered, 'Amen.'

Chapter Fifteen

'Come this way,' Krish said to the old woman. 'I know the exact layout of their house and garden and the cane fields. I've been here before. We'll go round the place and leave a trail of petrol as we go.' Krish snickered again.

It was a great plan. He and old Mrs Reddy were going to burn the cane fields. If his Ma's shack and the Van Niekerks' luxurious home got burned in the process, all the better, he thought. *Besides, maybe this will show Muniamma I mean business. She is going to marry Raj!*

'The fire will mean ruin for the white folk,' Mrs Reddy said maliciously and grinned. 'You know, don't you, that the mills are shut down and the burned cane will rot in the fields?'

'I know.' Krish smirked at his new partner. 'It'll serve them right for allowing their Indian workers to become Christians.'

'True...true,' Mrs Reddy said thoughtfully. 'This will also show those Christians that they can't go around spreading their Christian rubbish.' As she pondered about how she had seen them leaving for the sugar mill barracks and the conversation she had overheard, an uncontrollable anger filled her whole being. 'What a nerve!' she shouted and pressed the petrol can to her body.

'Shut up!' Krish demanded through clenched teeth. 'Do you want us to get caught?' Krish cursed the thought of having this worthless woman for a partner. *What a fool I've been to believe for one second that this feeble hag has special powers,* he thought. Krish stared at the old woman and rolled his eyes in utter disgust. 'Let's get this over with,' Krish growled.

Stealthily, the partners moved forward. Before they got far, Sparky started barking. 'That dumb dog!' Krish spat. 'I should have seen to him a long time ago.'

As they cautiously approached the Van Niekerks' immense garden where Grandmother and Muniamma worked, Krish nudged Mrs Reddy. 'Someone's coming...stay down!'

The two hid behind the thick cane, lying flat on the ground. Mr Van Niekerk continued walking around, shining his light. The beam from the torch flashed above their heads, and they both froze. He came closer, and just then Mrs Van Niekerk yelled, 'Do you see anything?'

'No!' he hollered back. His bristly moustache stuck straight out as he yelled at his wife. 'And shut that dog up...I can't hear myself think. Someone could be around, and I wouldn't be able to hear him.'

Krish thought of running. However, he had Mrs Reddy with him, and she would slow him down.

Besides, their containers couldn't be left; it would be too obvious that the fire was deliberate. Krish touched his pocket and remembered his knife. *I'll use it if I have to,* he vowed under his breath. *I'm not going to get caught!* He grasped the knife and got ready.

All the while Mrs Reddy had her face down in the dirt and was desperately wondering why she had ever devised this foolish plan in the first place. It would have been utterly simple to put a spell on Muniamma as Krish had suggested...a spell which would have made Muniamma fall wildly in love with Krish's partner.

Why didn't I do it? Mrs Reddy chided herself as she lay hiding. *Why didn't I concoct some spell? I certainly don't have to be out here in the mud trying to burn cane. There are easier ways to get even with Christians. And besides, I came to Isipingo to pray for my grandson.* She decided she would finish what they had come to do, but that would be the end of her association with Krish.

'Nothing's here,' Mr Van Niekerk yelled, interrupting Mrs Reddy's thoughts. 'That dumb dog has been tied up all day. No wonder he's barking like that! His noise is giving me a headache. Let's go home.'

'Do you smell something odd?' Mrs Van Niekerk asked, as her husband stepped over the rows in the garden.

'What do you mean?'

'I don't know...something smells strange around here.'

136

Mr Van Niekerk shook his head in disgust. 'You're always smelling something. You have the most sensitive nose of anyone I know.'

As the Van Niekerks left, old Mrs Reddy sighed in relief. Krish quickly flicked his knife closed and slipped it back into his pocket. 'Let's get out of here,' he whispered hoarsely. 'Who knows when they'll return, and besides, we're not quite finished. When we're done we need to get down to the bottom so we'll be in time to see a few shocked faces.'

Hours earlier, when she had overheard the Christians talking about going to the sugar mill barracks, Mrs Reddy had looked forward to that very thing. But now she wasn't so sure she wanted to hang around to see their faces. Her mind went again to the real reason she had come to Isipingo. She had fasted and prayed in the temple almost all this past week for her sick grandson. Desperately she clung onto hope for his life.

'I said...move it!' Krish shoved the old woman forward. She stumbled and caught herself on a thick stalk of cane. A huge rat scurried into the darkness.

Mrs Reddy turned and literally hissed at Krish. 'You have no idea who you're dealing with,' and it was almost like venom which spewed from the toothless mouth. 'I would be very careful if I were you!'

'Sure...sure,' Krish said sarcastically as he passed her on the fire breaker line and continued down the hill, walking proudly. 'Oooo, I'm scared, I'd better be careful...you might get me.' He laughed again at what he thought was a big joke.

137

The old woman did not respond. Her ominous silence should have been a warning to Krish, but he was too preoccupied with himself and his own revenge. He was totally unaware of this woman's powers.

Finally they reached the spot where they had first dribbled petrol. Krish took out his cigarette lighter. 'We're going down the hill before we start this fire.' Now his voice sounded serious, all sarcasm set aside. 'So listen carefully,' Krish continued. 'We'll separate here. There should be plenty of time to watch this cane burn when we get to the bottom.'

Old Mrs Reddy stood in front of Krish, staring at the dented can in her hands. It was too dark for Krish to see her expression of utter hate. She wanted to look up at this cocky individual and cast a spell which would make him squirm, but now was not the time.

Krish continued his instructions without realising his partner's thoughts. 'I heard this morning that Muniamma and all the rest of the Christians are returning from their little goodwill trip late tonight. I know just the spot where we can see them coming. Remember the place I pointed out to you earlier?'

Mrs Reddy nodded, keeping her head turned. Again she wondered why she had linked up with this foolish fellow. Tonight would soon be over, though. *When the vehicles carrying the Christians turn the corner, I'll shove this fool out into the road,* she planned. *He will have to take full responsibility. I have more important things on my mind,* and once again she thought of her sick grandchild at the sugar mill barracks. Fervently she began reciting prayers.

Old Mrs Reddy's love for her grandson went deep, and as she lumbered along she promised herself with an impassioned voice, 'No Christians will ever touch your life, not if I can help it—never!'

Chapter Sixteen

'Look!' Muniamma yelled from the back of the pick-up and pointed to the hills above Isipingo. 'What's happening?'

Sue, Lou and Kenny were sitting with her in the flat bed of the truck. They were all crowded together and covered over with blankets because of the cool night air. Muni sat straight up, and the wind blew hard in her face. She got to her knees, and Ken finally pulled her down. 'Careful, Muniamma. The truck's moving fast.'

'Look!' Muniamma screamed again. 'Fire!'

Ken looked over at the hills and shrugged his shoulders. 'I know. I saw it a while ago. Don't worry. Someone's just burning sugar cane.' He had to yell each word loudly because of the wind blowing in their faces.

Already the sweet pungent odour of the burned cane permeated the air. Flames shot high into the dark, starless sky.

'No one would burn cane tonight,' Muniamma cried hysterically. 'The mills are closed. And look, that's right around where Ma and I live!'

'Do you really think it's close to your house?' Sue asked. The twins looked worried.

The terrible thought that something awful was happening to Sparky made Muniamma shiver uncontrollably. Her prayer of faith, not more than an hour earlier, was totally forgotten. She waved frantically at the Mortons' van, which was following close behind the truck. She wanted them to notice the fire. But Mr Morton only waved in return and continued talking with his passengers.

Muniamma turned around and pounded on the back window of the truck. Aunt Sita looked, and Muni pointed to the hills. Sita's expression changed.

'Hurry!' Sita said to Uncle. 'The Van Niekerks wouldn't have started that. Something's wrong.'

By this time, everyone in both vehicles had noticed the fire. It was spreading. Muniamma felt panic rising within her, just like on the day of the flood when her mother and brothers had been killed.

'Sparky!' Muniamma kept screaming.

Lou grabbed her and hugged her close. 'I'm sure Sparky can take care of himself.'

'I tied him up,' Muniamma sobbed into Lou's shoulder. 'He can't get loose. It'll be my fault if he dies. Oh, Sparky...Sparky!'

None of the Morton children could bring comfort to Muniamma. She screamed and cried and finally pulled her knees up to her pointed chin. Hugging herself tightly, she dropped her head onto her knees and wept. Sheer determination kept her from going completely mad.

Sue, Lou and Kenny prayed frantically.

It seemed like for ever before the vehicles came to the bend in the road which led up to Poonamah and Muni's shack and the Van Niekerks' beautiful home. Great billows of heavy smoke continued filling the air. Everyone's eyes smarted.

Suddenly Uncle slammed on his brakes. Krish fell right onto the road, directly in front of the truck. Uncle tried his best to avoid hitting him. The truck swerved violently and finally came to an abrupt stop just a hair's breadth away.

Meanwhile, old Mrs Reddy chuckled to herself and cautiously remained hidden. *It would serve Krish right if he got run over,* she thought. Then she leaned forward to watch the expressions on each face as they stared at Krish who was standing angrily in the middle of the road.

She especially felt anxious to observe Poonamah and her granddaughter's expressions when they realised it was Krish who had caused the fire. 'This serves them right,' she muttered.

Suddenly, old Mrs Reddy noticed something for which she was totally unprepared. Sitting in the van, which had also come to an abrupt stop, were her son and daughter-in-law. She thought her eyes were deceiving her. 'This can't be!' she hissed.

She sneaked closer. Her mouth hung open showing its ugly toothless gums as she stared into the van window and saw her relatives with the missionaries and the precious baby, snuggled in the white woman's arms.

Old Mrs Reddy came closer, totally oblivious that

she was no longer hidden; that fact was the farthest thing from her mind. *How can this be?* she asked herself again. *Why would my relatives be in Isipingo with Christians? And why would that missionary be holding my grandchild?*

'Get out!' she screamed and flung herself at the van, pounding violently on the door. 'Get out!'

At the same time Krish began cursing and yelled, 'You pushed me!' and came at the old woman.

Also at that moment Muniamma screamed and jumped over the side of the truck. She landed hard on the ground, but she did not stop. She got up and ran towards her father. She instinctively knew he had caused the fire and was ultimately responsible for what was happening to Sparky. 'You've killed him!' she cried.

All these curses, demands and accusations were being hurled at the same time.

Just then, adding to the confusion, Raneesh and his parents arrived on some dilapidated old bikes. Raneesh threw his bike down and ran towards Muniamma while Mr and Mrs Naidoo hurried over to Uncle and Aunt Sita. 'Hey, we saw the fire and smoke. What's happening?'

Before Uncle had a chance to answer, Mr Morton scrambled out of the van and hollered to everyone, 'Look!' He pointed up the hill. The Van Niekerks' big Mercedes was coming down towards them with Sparky running out in front, as if he were leading.

'Sparky!' Muniamma screamed. In her relief she began to laugh and cry at once. Her head ached from all the tension, and all she wanted to do was hug her dog. She began running towards him with Raneesh at her side.

Grandmother had climbed out of the van when she had first spotted Krish. Immediately she grabbed Muni's arm and demanded, 'Wait!'

Sparky dashed right past Muniamma to Krish and crouched down, growling fiercely. Krish kicked at the dog and Sparky bit his baggy trousers and wouldn't let go.

Old Mrs Reddy was not paying any attention at all to the dog or Muniamma or Raneesh or the Mercedes or Krish. Instead, she leaned into the van and snatched the baby right out of Mary Morton's arms. 'How dare you touch this baby!' Her voice sounded like a snarl, and her lips curled back over the darkened skin of her gums. She stood still, angrily clutching the crying infant.

'Please!' her son and daughter-in-law begged. 'These people have saved our baby's life.'

Aunt Sita and Uncle interrupted. 'Quick! Get into the van.'

What Poonamah, Uncle and Aunt Sita had all noticed was the arrival of two uniformed policemen. They had been following the Van Niekerks and were now out of their patrol car and arresting Krish. The flashing light on top of their car cast weird shadows, and it made everyone's face look distorted.

Krish tried to jerk away, but a policeman held him firmly while Sparky continued pulling on his trousers. The screeching siren added to the confusion.

Krish pointed at old Mrs Reddy and yelled, 'She's

144

in on this too. She helped me start the fire.'

'Who?' one of the policemen demanded. 'Oh, sure...that old helpless woman sitting over there in that vehicle; the one holding the baby? You're sick, you are. Let's get him out of here.'

After putting him in handcuffs, they roughly shoved him into the enclosed back seat of the police car and locked the door. Krish's face looked grotesque as he glared out of the bullet-proof window. First he stared at Muniamma and then his Ma, Raneesh, the Morton family, Aunt Sita and Uncle, the Reddys and especially at old Mrs Reddy. Then his eyes finally settled back on Muniamma, and his hatred grew.

Muniamma did not even notice. She was on her knees hugging her dog. Sparky licked her thoroughly all over her face and lapped up her tears.

'You're a hero!' Muniamma said breathlessly.

'You're right,' Mr Van Niekerk interrupted. 'That dog of yours alerted us to danger. At first, we found nothing, but that old mutt would not shut up. So...we kept looking and eventually we both smelled petrol.'

Mrs Van Niekerk nodded proudly.

'Anyway, my wife let the dog free and I immediately radioed the surrounding farmers and the authorities. Dozens of people came to help, and it wasn't long before the fire was completely under control.'

Mr Van Niekerk stopped in the middle of his explanation and thoughtfully touched his wiry moustache. 'Those fire breaker lines really helped in

She was on her knees hugging her dog.

containing the fire, but what still seems strange to me is how the wind changed and began blowing in the direction of the fire. The fire actually burned itself out. I'd call it nothing short of a miracle.'

'That's right,' Mrs Van Niekerk said with deep emotion, 'though we also need to give credit to this dog. He's the one who alerted us.'

'Oh, Sparky, congratulations,' Ken said, and he and the twins rushed forward and knelt beside Muniamma, Raneesh and her dog. Sue and Lou hugged Muni, and all three girls giggled nervously as Sparky wagged his tail and nestled in close. Ken and Raneesh smiled at each other.

'He knows he's the hero,' Sue said.

Grandmother walked over to the huddled group and looked at Muniamma and her friends. 'Let the dog have his moment of glory; he deserves it.'

Muniamma looked up lovingly at her grandmother. 'Oh, Ma!'

But, suddenly, a dark shadow descended over Grandmother's face, and she turned back to the policemen. 'What's going to happen to my son?' she asked, her voice full of sorrow.

'Well,' Mr Van Niekerk answered before the uniformed men could respond. 'I hope he's going to jail. Don't worry, he is not going to cause any more trouble, neither to you, nor to me. That's why I came away from my farm at a crucial time like this. It was obvious that dog was on the trail of the culprit. I wanted to come along and identify this man.' Mr Van Niekerk pointed right at Krish, who was slumped over dejectedly in the back seat of the patrol car.

The pudgy officer interrupted, 'It seems we have all the evidence we need. He'll be put in jail, pending a thorough investigation.'

'He will be allowed to have visitors, won't he?' Mr Morton asked anxiously. He was standing back with his wife at his side. Mary Morton was holding Shelley, and Kathie stood behind them. Missionary Morton continued, 'You see, this man has caused everyone lots of trouble, but I still think there's hope for him. The longer I live here in South Africa, the more I realise God is in the business of doing miracles.'

The police officers looked at each other and shrugged. 'That's up to you,' they said to Mr Morton. 'I'm sure he'll be allowed to have visitors.'

'We want to come too,' Aunt Sita and Uncle said from the van.

Mr Van Niekerk frowned at the police officers. It was obvious they did not understand this group of Christians.

Grandmother sighed and a tear trickled down her dark, wrinkled face. She quickly wiped it away. 'My son has a partner. Have you found him?'

'No, but we will,' they promised.

While all this was going on, old Mrs Reddy stayed in the van, holding her precious grandson. She too had tears in her eyes, but it was because she had heard snatches of the story about the baby's convulsions. Her son and daughter-in-law were also trying to explain something about evil spirits. None of it made sense to the old woman because all she could think about was how thankful she was her grand-

148

child was alive. She knew she'd want the details tomorrow, but for now she felt content to cuddle the baby to her breast.

Sparky barked loudly and his noise seemed to throw everyone into immediate action. As Muniamma rose to her feet, an indescribable calm enveloped her. She smiled at her friends. Each smiled in return, but there was something special in Raneesh's tender look.

Chapter Seventeen

Back in their old shack with the heavy odour of burned cane lingering in the air, Muniamma snuggled farther down into the bed, close to Grandmother.

Faint moonlight filtered through the banana leaves outside, tracing dancing patterns across the walls of their cramped one-room home. Muni smiled to herself, remembering how she used to think the shadows were the arms of the terrifying goddess Kali reaching out to clutch her.

Sparky was panting, and he flopped his big head onto the edge of the sagging mattress. 'Sparky, my friend,' she whispered into his ear. 'You're my brave hero!' She ran her fingers through his straggly hair, but he pulled away.

'Come back here, boy,' she teased quietly, shaking her head back and forth as she whispered.

Sparky yawned and lay down on the cool floor next to Muniamma's side of the bed. Leaning over the edge, she let her hand rest lovingly on Sparky's neck. 'You were my only friend when I came here a year ago as an orphan. Remember, Sparky?

Remember how it was?'

For long moments Muniamma allowed her mind to drift over the past year. Visions of Kali flashed through her mind, and she shivered, remembering the curse. Then the truth of how she and Ma had become Christians overpowered these disturbing thoughts, and the shivers were replaced by a warm, cosy feeling as if the thin blanket had been replaced by a thick, fluffy one.

Then dreamy thoughts of the Mortons and Raneesh settled over her, making her feel even more cosy. 'I want Raneesh to become a special friend,' Muni confided to her dog. 'A very special friend!' Sparky began to breathe heavily and every once in a while his feet would jerk as if he were running. 'Sleep on, faithful one,' she said.

Just as Muniamma was about to drift into sleep, it felt as if an intruder had come and yanked her right out of bed and plopped her down behind a crumbling tombstone, leaving her cold and exposed. Krish and Raj seemed to stand over her, grinning, while old Mrs Reddy cackled and her son lurked nearby with a huge butcher's knife. She knew it was all in her imagination, but it seemed real.

Rolling over onto her back she stared up at the corrugated ceiling, trying desperately to relax. Once again she looked around their ordinary room. The soft moonlight made the cobwebs in the corners look like silver threads. The place on the ceiling that Mr Morton had patched months earlier was still dry. She took a long, deep breath. The lingering smoke of the burned cane made her throat feel parched.

Then, as she had done several times that day, Muniamma gently touched the dressing above her left eye. 'Oh God, who made the sunrise and the moonlight,' she prayed, 'one minute I am trusting you, and the next minute I'm not. Please help me.'

She paused and let her fingers trace the outline of the bandage. She took another deep breath and continued quietly, 'Next time I'm knocked down by a big problem, a jacaranda tree or a Mr Reddy or even a big old fat Raj, please help me to remember that you are there. And every time I see this scar on my forehead or even feel it, help me to stop and think. I want it to become my secret reminder.'

'What are you mumbling about at this late hour?' Grandmother complained. 'It must be well past midnight and we have a lot of work to do tomorrow.'

Muni turned towards her grandmother and grasped her hand. 'I know, Ma, but I need to talk. Last week I wasn't ready to be baptised, and I shamed all of you by running away. I guess I especially made God sad because I wasn't trusting him.'

'Don't worry, child. God understands.' Lovingly she squeezed Muniamma's hand in return.

'But Ma—I really do want to get baptised this time. I know that no matter what happens God is with me. He is even helping me with my fear of my father and his awful plans. And for some reason I know God is going to take care of everything. I just know it!'

'That's good, child...that's good.' Ma's voice sounded funny, as if she were falling back to sleep.

Soon Grandmother began snoring, and the noise was louder than ever before. She wanted to watch Ma's lips as they sputtered and flapped but was simply too tired and sore to prop herself up and take a closer look.

Muniamma rolled onto her side and pulled the thin blanket up to her dimpled chin. She had been considering reminding Grandmother that next Sunday was her birthday. *That can wait,* she thought longingly. *Oh, but what I'd really love to do is get baptised on my fourteenth birthday.*

Slowly a smile played on Muniamma's lips as she drifted into a restful sleep, safe in her heavenly Father's care.

THE END

Author's Note

I hope you have read the first two books in the Tales of Muniamma Series, *Child of Destiny* and *Escape from the Darkness*, because you will realise that this book continues Muniamma's story.

So many incidents prompted the writing of these books. While my husband, Geoff, and I and our daughters were missionaries in South Africa we worked among Indian people from a Hindu background. We were like the missionary family in this series, who had so much to learn.

Our Indian friends were tremendous examples and were very patient in helping us to understand their ways. I wanted to share their struggles and triumphs with you; that's why I wrote this story.

Here are a few real-life situations which touched our hearts:

* A girl who had a curse put on her before she was born. Through many miracles God delivered this girl, and today she is a strong Christian leader.

* A young boy who was beaten each week because he wanted to attend Sunday school to learn about

Jesus. Today the parents are Christians.

* A girl who was made to stand in the corner of her home for hours because she would no longer pray to the family idol. Today this girl's mother is a Christian, and her father is attending the Christian meetings.

* A mother who was attacked with a butcher knife by a relative because she dared to become a Christian. God miraculously saved her from being killed. Today many of her family members know the Lord.

* A girl who had a spell put on her to make her fall in love with a certain man. Through the power of prayer, God broke that spell and the girl did not marry him.

* A teenage boy who was overcome by evil spirits. God delivered this boy, and today a church meets in his home.

As you read the previous pages, think of the real people behind the story. Each one has struggles and serious times of doubt, but they are all learning to trust God. You, too, may be experiencing problems. God can meet you at your very point of need. We have a loving heavenly Father and he is still in the business of doing miracles.

My prayer is that you grow in your walk with Jesus as Muniamma does in the pages of this book.

Connie Griffith

155

The Africa Evangelical Fellowship

This book is published in association with AEF. The Africa Evangelical Fellowship is an international evangelical mission. It had its beginnings in the challenge of missionary outreach in South Africa in the 1880s. Together with Spencer Walton, Andrew Murray was God's man to accept this challenge, and the work of the South Africa General Mission began in Capetown in 1889. Andrew Murray was the president of the SAGM until his death in 1917. Since then, over 1300 missionaries, among them Mrs Connie Griffith, have served in 13 different countries of southern Africa under the SAGM and AEF, as the mission has been known since 1961. Today, over 360 missionaries are still active in Africa serving with AEF, establishing churches and working with those churches established under past ministries. For more information about their work, please contact them at their International Office, 35 Kingfisher Court, Hambridge Road, Newbury RG14 5SJ, England.

The AEF has hundreds of opportunities for both long and short term service in evangelism, church planting, education, administration, medical work, youth work and other practical fields.

Other AEF offices are:

Australia:
PO Box 292
Castle Hill
New South Wales 2154

Canada:
470 McNicoll Avenue
Willowdale
Ontario M2H 2E1

USA:
PO Box 2896
Boone
North Carolina 28607

Zimbabwe:
PO Box 8164
Causeway
Harare

South Africa:
PO Box 23913
Claremont 7735

New Zealand:
PO Box 1390
Invercargill

United Kingdom:
30 Lingfield Road
Wimbledon
London SW19 4PU

Continental Europe:
5 Rue de Meautry
94500 Campigny-sur-
    Marne
France

Child Of Destiny

by Connie Griffith

Muniamma was hiding in a banana grove on the hillside above her grandmother's house. The pain of losing her mother and brothers was still there.

Her sorrow mingled with fear as she thought of Grandmother's religion—devotion to the mysterious goddess Kali. Living for Kali involved strange happenings. Not like the God that her aunt and uncle had discovered, 'the God who made the sun rise'.

But where could he be found? And what would Grandmother do if Muniamma went looking for him?

CONNIE GRIFFITH weaves events that have actually happened into an exciting and at times moving narrative for children. She lives in North Carolina with her husband—the executive director of the American Council of the AEF—and their two daughters. For eight years they were AEF missionaries in South Africa, where this story is set.

K
Kingsway Publications

Escape From The Darkness

by Connie Griffith

Muniamma's heart was heavy as she thought back over the past year. So much had happened. The flood had started it, sweeping away her home and family. Sparky, her dog, was all she had left.

And then there was Kali, the goddess that had more to do with fear than love. How could Muniamma get away from her?

Now she was ill, so Grandmother was going to take her to the temple. But it was not from that strange place that healing was going to come.

CONNIE GRIFFITH weaves events that have actually happened into an exciting and at times moving narrative for children. She lives in North Carolina with her husband—the executive director of the American Council of the AEF—and their two daughters. For eight years they were AEF missionaries in South Africa, where this story is set.

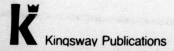

Kingsway Publications